WHERE THE PAST BELONGS

WHERE THE PAST BELONGS

AN ANGELICA AND ASH TIME TRAVEL ADVENTURE

ROBERT J. MCCARTER

LITTLE HUMMINGBIRD PUBLISHING

Where the Past Belongs

An Angelica and Ash Time Travel Adventure

Copyright © 2020 by Robert J. McCarter

Except as permitted under the Copyright Act of 1976, this book may not be reproduced in whole or in part in any manner.

This book is a work of fiction. Names, places, and incidents are either products of the author's imagination or used fictitiously. Any resemblance to actual events or persons, living or dead, is entirely coincidental.

Cover images

- Infinity Vector by Vecteezy
- Clock: ©Depositphto.com, hayatikayhan
- Seattle Skyline: ©Depositphto.com, mauromod
- Dog: ©Depositphto.com, eriklam
- Cat: ©Depositphto.com, YAYImages

Version 1.0, December 2020

ISBN: 978-1-941153-52-9

Visit Robert's website at: RobertJMcCarter.com

Published by:

Little Hummingbird Publishing

P.O. Box 23518

Flagstaff, AZ 86002

❀ Created with Vellum

This one is dedicated to Tyra. She was an adorable rescue mutt, a highly skilled escape artist, an amazing companion, and exactly what I needed during some very difficult and lonely years. And to all the other dogs that have made my life so very much richer.

At least 10% of proceeds from this book will be donated to animal charities.

WARNING: The following story contains a twisting time travel plot and is unapologetically sentimental when it comes to the animals we humans share our lives with. The author and the publisher can not be held responsible that if, after reading this novel, you feel a very strong desire to find an animal in need and take very, very good care of it.

PART ONE

MY LOVE'S PAST

CHAPTER ONE

I KNOW you're not going to believe this. Hell, I have trouble believing it and I lived it. So I'm just going to come out and say it.

Time travel is real.

Yup, real as you or me, but not what you think it is. Or, rather, not *who* you think it is. Or... It's hard to explain, so I guess I'm just going to have to tell you the story. And like any time-travel story, the "beginning" and the "end" are relative, subjective, but I'll start where it begins for me.

My name is Ashton Bach, but everyone calls me Bach. When I was in junior high, I lobbied for the nickname of "Ash," which I thought was cool, but that fell flat next to my last name, the same name as the famous German composer. Which is ironic, seeing how I am the least musically inclined person you will ever meet.

I just turned fifty years old and after what I've been through in the last few... well, I want to call them days, but we *are* talking time travel here, so let me try that again. After the last few days of my subjective experience skipping around the timeline, I feel a hell of a lot older.

Well, older in that I am tired and worn out, scratched and bruised. But I also feel younger, like I'm seeing the world as it really is for the very first time.

It's much weirder and much more wonderful than I imagined.

And while it may seem like I'm meandering a bit, trying to find my way into the story (spoiler alert: I am) those pieces of information are actually important. I am a fifty-year-old geek who everyone calls Bach but wished he was called Ash.

Got it?

Okay, here we go.

IT STARTED ON A SATURDAY. I was at home working. It's what I do. Well, I play a lot of video games and I go bowling on Sundays (kind of my church), and I volunteer at the humane society helping to take care of dogs on Monday. You know, since I work on Saturdays, I take Mondays off.

Yeah. I am a bit out of sync with the world. I bet you are getting that about me already. Another important thing to remember.

Anyway, I was working on a Saturday afternoon. Which I love. No one calls me. No one bothers me. I had Journey cranked (remember, I'm not a kid although I can sure act like one) on my smart speaker and was standing at my desk typing away.

Well, programming. That's what I do. I make electrons dance and people pay me to do it. I'm a programmer for hire helping corporations fulfill their avaristic dreams via technology. It's kind of like getting paid to play video games—except for all the damn meetings, copious messages on Slack, phone calls, and endless emergencies and... well, you get the idea. I may love my job, but it's still a J O B.

Okay, so middle-aged dude (me) at a standing desk, long greying hair pulled back into a ponytail dressed in shorts, a faded Bob Seger concert T-shirt, and some cheap flip-flops.

My office is an ode to my era of geek with things like a vintage *Star Wars* poster of X-wings battling in front of the death star, and an original *Raiders of the Lost Ark* movie poster. Also bookshelves filled with first-edition hardbacks with names like Tolkien, Heinlein, Asimov, and the like. Other shelves with DVDs, Blu-rays, and games. It's all a bit messy and a bit chaotic with no unifying theme except for "middle-aged geek" and that's the way I like it.

I'm typing. I'm mouthing the words I've been hearing Steve Perry sing for decades. It's my fun Saturday everyone-leave-me-alone groove, when a bunch of things happen at once.

During a break between songs, I hear some honking outside. My desk faces away from the window, so I turn around and glance out at the busy road and see a tall homeless guy standing there on the sidewalk, swaying like he's having some kind of religious experience... or maybe he's just starving. He's way overdressed for Phoenix in a dirty and tattered trench coat, but at least he's rocking a ponytail, a mess though it may be.

Right as a new song starts up, my smart speaker goes mute and I turn back around.

I hear my front door open.

A dog barks loudly, an urgent "danger danger, Will Robinson" kind of bark, and I hear the telltale click of nails on my laminate floors.

I take a step to the side so my monster monitor is not occluding my view of the door.

And then the dog is in my office. A corgi with pointed ears, short legs, and a lovely tan-and-white coat. Its big brown eyes connect with mine and I swear the dog knows me.

I know dogs. I love dogs. I'm currently living in an apartment, having recently moved to Phoenix to keep an eye on my aging parents, and I can't have one here.

That's the other thing I do a lot. Help my parents out. Yard work. Doctors' appointments. Making sure they are okay. I'm their only child and it's the right thing to do.

But back to our story and that corgi in my office. So I know what it feels like to look into the eyes of a dog. You can connect instantly. It can be deep. And this is that and a whole bunch more.

The corgi is panting, looking like it's been running as fast as it can on those short legs.

I open my mouth, planning to say something doggy-adorable like, "How'd you get in here, you beautiful boy?" but the dog beats me to it.

He barks and then says....

Wait. It's about to get weird, but stay with me, okay. Remember that I said time travel is real but it wasn't what or *who* you thought it was.

So he barks, opens his mouth, and says, "Come with me if you want to live."

Well, the dog doesn't exactly "speak," no moving of the mouth, but I hear those words in my head.

And no, the dog doesn't sound anything like Arnold Schwarzenegger in *Terminator 2*. In fact, the dog's speaking voice sounds more female than male, the kind of voice you would expect from a young, well-educated woman with a high-brow English accent.

So I assumed wrong. The dog is a girl. I also assumed that the dog wasn't telepathic, so zero out of two for me.

And yeah, T2 is something of a landmark movie for me. I was twenty-two when it came out. It was the best movie I had ever seen. I've probably watched it fifty times by now. I can say a lot of the lines from memory.

And I am geek enough to know that the phrase originated with *The Terminator*, but I think it was Schwarzenegger's robotic delivery of it that embedded it into our cultural zeitgeist.

So, I'm confronted with a telepathic corgi uttering the ultimate movie catch line (for a dude my age, that is), so what do I do?

I follow the dog, of course.

And as I do, I clearly hear the honking of horns and then the crunch of metal. I'm in my modest living room, which is not much more than a comfy brown couch, huge flat-screen TV, and a gaming rig. I glance back into my office to see an old red Chevy pickup crash through the wall and take out my standing desk, my computer, and my beautiful, ultra-wide 49" monitor.

Remember, my desk faces the room, not the window.

I wouldn't have seen the out of control truck hop the curb and head towards my building. If the speaker hadn't glitched out I wouldn't have heard it over Steve Perry telling me "Don't Stop Believin'."

And as much as it hurts to see my beautiful desk and monitor and computer turned into so much garbage, I realize the talking dog had been speaking the truth and had just saved my life.

I didn't need any more convincing than that. I followed the dog.

CHAPTER TWO

I DON'T LIKE PHOENIX. It's hot. It's a sprawling waste-land of strip malls and suburbia that has taken over the hot desert floor of the Valley of the Sun.

My last place of residence was Seattle. Yeah, the constant clouds take some getting used to, but there is water and you can grow things, and the city, while sprawling, has its own funky vibe that is so much fun.

Phoenix is where I was born. I only came back to take care of my parents.

Okay, well, maybe it was more than that. Like losing my wife to cancer and having everything about Seattle remind me of her. We had met there, fell in love there, and lived there for over two decades.

So, yeah, while I was taking care of my parents physically, they were taking care of me emotionally.

I'm a gangly geek who spends his days on a computer making a living and loves to spend his nights on a computer shooting zombies (or aliens, or anything, really). How am I supposed to find another woman like Mia that will embrace my geeky self?

And even that feels foreign to me, the "find another woman" part. That is there, but I'm more in the phase where I can't imagine being happy—or truly functional—without her, even though she's been gone for two years.

All of this is just more salient details about me that you need to know.

So, back to the telepathic corgi that just saved my life with the Terminator series catch phrase.

I find her on the grass outside my apartment complex looking like any other dog. She is sitting there panting in the hot sun and scratches at her pointy ear with her back claw.

I can smell oil and my ears are still ringing from the sound of the crash.

And then I smell smoke.

Shit.

The apartment complex isn't at all inspiring. Three long buildings two stories high encased in faux adobe with a pool nestled between two of the buildings. The place is about to burn down. I should do something about that, right? But what about this dog, I don't want to lose her. I mean, she's a telepathic dog that just saved my life. But my neighbors.

"Don't go anywhere," I say to the dog, holding my palm up. "Please. I'll be right back."

I pull my phone from my pocket, dial 911, and run into the apartment complex and start banging on doors.

I could afford a house, being a bit slinger for hire pays me pretty well, but I don't want to put roots down. Although I have discovered that I may be a bit too old for apartment living. Too much noise. Too many people. But it is what it is, and I would hate myself if I didn't try to help my neighbors.

Twenty minutes later, the fire department is on site and my whole apartment building is engulfed in flames and the neighbors are warned and the corgi is gone.

For a moment there, a thin little moment, I thought this was the universe's rather twisted way of making up for what happened to Mia. Like it was saying, "Sorry about the love of your life and her cancer, but here's a telepathic dog that just saved your life for you to hang out with."

But not even that.

And what if it had all been my imagination? Maybe I hadn't closed my door properly and the dog had wandered in at the same time my smart speaker glitched. Maybe the dog had barked and my subconscious had heard the wreck happening and made me think the dog was talking so I would move my ass.

And that made it even worse.

Not finding the dog, I look around and it's a scene, I'll tell you that. Three engines spraying water and an assemblage of about fifteen firefighters. There's half a dozen cops trying to corral the civilians and deal with the snarl of traffic on the road, the fire engines blocking a lane, and the lookie-loos slowing down to gawk at the tragedy.

I flop onto the grass and watch the fire department spray water on what used to be my place of residence. The heat from the fire is like a wall of hot that is much worse than the summer sun. I'm twenty yards away and it's like I just stuck my head into an oven on broil.

Other neighbors are wandering around, a glazed look of shock in their eyes. And if I looked in the mirror, I'm sure I'd look that way too.

As I stare at the flames, I realize that my life is in ruins. Again. Not only is my desk and computing rig gone, but my vintage *Star Wars* poster, my antique Tonka truck collection—the awesome old metal ones—, my DVDs and Blu-rays, my—

And then it hits me. I had kept a stash of Mia's favorite clothes. When it got really bad, I would unseal the big Tupperware tub I kept them in and just breathe in her scent, a bit musky and a bit flowery. For a second it would be like she was not gone, like my life was not ruined, like I was not alone.

It was only a moment and only a trick, but the fire would take that from me too. The desk and other things were replaceable, just things, but what I had left of Mia was not.

I twiddle with the gold band I still wear on my left hand. At least I still have that.

The sun is setting to the west and I figure I'd better call my folks, tell them what happened, go stay with them until I can find another place, but I hesitate.

While I have a fertile imagination, there was something about that corgi. Something about her eyes. I didn't really imagine it, did I? As I think on it, I can't remember her mouth moving. I connected with those eyes and heard her voice but she looked like a dog the whole time.

And then she is there nuzzling her way under my arm, panting, her doggy breath smell filling my nose. Suddenly things aren't so bad anymore.

"There you are," I say with a smile, petting her silky fur. I don't care if I had imagined her talking or not, it is clear what I need in my life is a dog. One that needs a home.

But this corgi is well cared for. I get on my knees and look her over and see a few things. First, that look of deep intelligence is still there, like she is seeing into my soul, like she knows me. Second, she isn't wearing a collar.

"Who are you, girl?" I ask.

Those penetrating brown eyes look deep into my soul, she stops panting, and I hear a female voice in my head say, "My name is Angelica Huston. Come with me if you want to live again."

She starts panting again and trots off, away from the flashing red lights and the heat of the fire.

I follow. Of course I do.

CHAPTER THREE

"LIKE THE ACTRESS?" I ask, catching up to the corgi who is trotting down the sidewalk away from my burning apartment complex, the heat from the fire rapidly fading. She may have short legs, but she can move when she wants to. "Like from *The Grifters* or *Prizzi's Honor?*"

Right. I've got a telepathic dog that just saved my life on my hands and all I can think of to ask is about her name.

She gives a sharp bark and starts trotting faster down the sidewalk. We've passed a couple more apartment buildings similar to mine and are now walking past homes that were probably built in the nineties with stucco walls and terracotta shingles in mute earth tones. The yards are desert-appropriate with mostly gravel and a few hardy trees and some cacti.

"I knew I liked you, Ashton Bach," she says. "While my real name is unpronounceable by apes like you, I am glad the great actress's—whose name I adopted—more significant works are known to you. Except, I do spell 'Angelica' with a 'g' not a 'j'. Just seems more sensible."

So the dog is telepathic. She knows who I am. And she watches movies and has a thing for Anjelica (with a "j") Huston.

What...?

I've been known to imbibe at times. A beer here and there. A joint now and then. I even tried magic mushrooms once—spoiler alert, too much vomiting for me—but I had never hallucinated a talking dog.

Because I must be hallucinating this, right?

I mean, I get it. Angelica Huston is a fine actress and under used. She is best known for her portrayal of Morticia Addams in *The Addams Family* movies, which is clearly not her best work, but I am by no means the kind of fan this dog seems to be. Or maybe I have some subconscious thing for her that I never realized and the stress of this accident and losing my last remnants of Mia has forced a little psychological break and I'm really running around Phoenix after a stray corgi, all the good parts just going on in my mind.

I shrug my shoulders and walk fast to keep up with the dog. We leave the nineties houses behind and turn onto a smaller street with older homes that are more varied, and then turn down a narrow alley. The dog slips between two broken boards in an aging privacy fence and I'm alone.

I can hear the distant sound of traffic and smell the heady scent of flowers from someone's yard, but that's it. I'm alone in an alley wondering whether I should trespass onto a stranger's yard to follow my hallucination.

And I just stand there.

This is trauma, pure and simple. This is unresolved grief and me living too isolated a life in Phoenix. Corgis don't talk to humans telepathically.

The second time, she had said, "Come with me if you want to live *again*." That's not the line from the movie. What had she meant by "again"? Or rather what had my subconscious meant by "again"?

I have no idea where I am. Why would my subconscious bring me here unless I am so far gone that I need serious help?

"Well, come on then, ape," Angelica Huston says in my head, her head sticking through the hole in the fence. "I don't have all day." And then those eyes seem to be looking deeper into me and she does this bark that sounds way more like a laugh than a normal bark.

Her head disappears and I stand there chewing on my lip, looking around, making sure no one is coming, and then I do it.

Well, "do it" makes it sound like I'm some well-muscled dude from a Nike ad. I'm not. I'm tall and skinny and have the upper body strength of someone who spends their days on a computer.

What I do do is climb over the fence, managing to scrape my knee, cut my hand, and rip my shorts, but I make it over and only land hard enough to jar my teeth and not break anything.

I open my mouth to speak but see the spaceship.

Well, it's either that or a giant silver dog bone sitting in the half-dead, half-weedy yard of what must be an unoccupied house.

The dog is standing by the bone or ship or whatever it is. It dwarfs her and is about fifteen feet long and six feet wide where it flares out at the ends. It is reflective, looking like it's made out of metal, and I can see a distorted version of myself gawking.

I'm squished so I look short, and the dog, who is closer, looks giant next to me.

There are so many questions. I mean, could I really be hallucinating something this bizarre without some kind of chemical aid? But on the other hand (or paw, as it were) can this be real?

"I... Umm... You...." I mumble like an idiot, sounding like I don't know how to talk and am not a well-trained engineer. "What is going on?"

As I write this, I don't even know how to refer to my companion. If I call her "the dog" or "the corgi" that seems to fall short of what I am experiencing with this creature. If I call her by her name, Angelica Huston, then you might summon the image of a woman with black hair, prominent cheekbones, and her ever-present bangs.

Suffice it to say that in the moment I am way more confused than that.

"Are you an alien?" I ask.

Okay, with all the sci-fi movies and books I've inhaled, that took me way longer than it should have.

"Duh," Angelica says in my head. "I'm from Sirius. The dog star, you know."

"And... what... why...?" I'm back to incoherent mumbling.

She pads over and licks my scraped knee and sits down and I find myself sitting down too. Did she make me do that?

What remains of the grass is dry and poking into my legs quite uncomfortably.

"Can you please just come with me?" she asks, her feminine voice crystal clear in my head although she is just sitting there panting in the heat. "I will level with you, Ashton Bach. I just got promoted and you are my first mission in my new role. I promise things will become clear, but for now we need to go."

I nod. I am not really signaling my agreement, it's more like my head isn't on properly and it bounces up and down because there is nothing else it can do.

An iris opens in the side of the ship and the dog trots in, jumping up and landing inside the ship and disappearing.

There is a brief pause while I sit there quite convinced that I have lost it and will soon be spending the rest of my life as a ward of the state. I mean, my hallucination is a talking dog that just got promoted and I am her mission. If that isn't the kind of thing you get locked up for, I don't know what is.

But then I can see her looking at me, those deep brown eyes look more than a little sad.

"This will help you, Ashton Bach," she says. "And I've got air-conditioning."

"But... but my parents," I say, suddenly thinking of my responsibilities here. "I need to check on them tonight."

Angelica cocks her head and I swear she has a smile on her doggy face. "Don't worry, Ashton Bach, I will get you back in time."

And something clicks in my head. If I'm crazy, I might as well see how deep the rabbit hole goes. If I'm not crazy, it's a freaking telepathic alien dog with a spaceship.

I move and I move fast.

CHAPTER FOUR

THE INSIDE of a dog-star alien's spaceship is all rounded corners and soft surfaces. Which is good because there is plenty of crawling for someone my size. This spaceship is definitely built for those with four legs, not bipedal apes like myself.

Wait. When did I start thinking of myself as an ape? Alien telepathic dogs can really get in your head. Literally. But I guess I see the rationale from her perspective. We evolved from apes. She evolved from canines. I'm an ape. She's a dog.

But still, it's strange, isn't it?

The surfaces inside that dog's spaceship are grey and undecorated. The ship has this loamy, earthy scent to it that is rather pleasant. And, I am happy to report, there is air-conditioning, although I never see any vents or any delivery mechanism for it.

Angelica Huston leads me to what must be the bridge. It's just tall enough for me to sit comfortably and just big enough for me and this low platform in the middle of the room. It has four small holes in it and she climbs on and inserts her paws, sniffing at a stalk that rises in front of the platform.

The scent of the room changes, but I can't really tell you quite how. It's loamier maybe, definitely more intense. I get the distinct impression that the stalk she is sniffing is emitting odors that are more suited to canines than apes.

The curved front of the room changes from bland grey to a grainy black-and-white view of the single-story home in front of the ship.

I don't feel anything, no movement whatsoever, but the black-and-white image changes and soon we are looking at the roof of the house and then the house is far below us and then Phoenix is laid out in an orderly grid that is barely disturbed by the occasional craggy hill, and then the view of Phoenix is sliding down off the screen and is gone.

"Where are we going?" I ask.

Angelica seems to be busy, her paws making small movements in the holes, her nose twitching rapidly, while her eyes take in the view of the Earth below us.

She is flying the ship. Obviously. That is what that platform is all about. No hands. No fingers. So these dog aliens developed technology that they can use with their paws. And the smells, well that must be since their olfactory senses are way better than ours, they have technology to communicate information via smell.

She turns and glances at me, her eyes looking intense this time and I feel my stomach tighten. I'm no longer considering hallucination. I'm all the way in. This is real. And with that look, I'm wondering what the hell I got myself into.

"We are going to Seattle," she says in my head. "But 'where' is not the right question to ask, Ashton Bach."

We must be high now because the view below us is partially occluded by clouds and even more toylike than from an airplane.

"What is the right question?" I ask.

I swear she smiles again. "'When' is the right question."

It takes a moment for my strained brain to put it together. She used the terminator catch-phrase. She just told me she would "get me back in time." She's taking us to Seattle.

"You are a time traveler," I gasp.

She gives a joyful bark and wags her tail. "My species are the *only* time travelers."

We're going to Seattle. In the past. She also said, "Come with me if you want to live *again*."

"Mia," I say, tears forming in my eyes, but Angelica Huston isn't paying attention to me anymore.

We are so high, I can see the curvature of the Earth. If I'm not hallucinating, I just became an astronaut. And then I can't even think about that most geeky of milestones because the view of the Earth changes.

It's hard to explain. It's not like when in the first Superman movie, Christopher Reeve's Superman made the Earth spin backwards to turn back time, it's more like the Earth shudders, goes out of focus for a few breathless moments, and then shudders back into focus.

While this is happening, I feel like I'm shuddering myself. Like I'm going out of focus and then I'm shuddering back into focus. It smells like plastic is burning and my skin prickles like a bad case of the hives are about to descend. My already rattled brain is further rattled and I'm glad I skipped lunch, otherwise it would have been all over the soft grey floor of Angelica Huston's spaceship.

And then we are plunging down towards Seattle, the verdant land and so much water, the city bracketed by Puget Sound and Lake Washington with Mount Rainier to the south, the land around the city thick with forests. Even on the grainy black-and-white display it's spectacular, but all I can think of is my beloved Mia whole and healthy.

CHAPTER FIVE

"WHEN ARE WE? What is our mission? Why me?" I ask. I had more questions. Believe me, I had more questions, but sitting on the bridge of the alien dog's spaceship watching the Earth rise up, getting a glimpse of the Space Needle, watching as we plunged into a rather plain Seattle suburb just west of Lake Washington, and watching as we land in someone's backyard was enough to stifle all of those other questions.

I didn't feel motion, ever—except for that shudder thing when, I presume, we were time traveling. The ship must have inertial dampers or something—either that or I was hallucinating.

No. Not hallucinating. Let's see how deep the rabbit hole goes.

So, as we descend, I did my best to collect myself and came up with my oh-so-obvious when/what/why question.

Angelica Huston, still on the canine control platform,

turns to me and says, "1984. Getting your life back. Why not?"

It takes me a moment to unpack that.

We had time traveled back to 1984, which gave me a bit of a shudder. George Orwell's dystopian future did not come to pass, but a sci-fi geek like me is going to notice a date like that.

Our mission was "getting my life back" and I had no idea how we could do that in 1984.

And as to why me, the answer was "why not?"

By the time I had unpacked it all, I'm outside the spaceship chasing a corgi through a damp Seattle evening, quite underdressed in my shorts and Bob Seger T-shirt. But hey, at least folks these days will be a lot more familiar with the marvelous Mr. Seger.

But how do I get my life back in 1984? Mia will be all of twelve, and if getting my life back doesn't have something to do with her, what kind of world is this?

The neighborhood looks like an old one, with smaller single-story homes, some built out of cinderblocks, some stick built, most with attached one-car garages. But then I have to twist my mind around. It's 1984. These could be newer homes. This is Seattle, so trees are large and verdant, hedges abound, and the perfumed scent of flowers fills my nose.

I take a deep breath. I may have been born in the desert, but this is what hope smells like to me. My skin drinks in the damp air and I feel more energy in my limbs than I have had in a while.

A few minutes later, I'm in an alley that runs between two rows of houses faced with wooden privacy fences, tree branches are arching over, and a sudden bit of mist descends, making the rather mundane feel rather mystical.

I can't see Angelica and I speed up my pace and then suddenly I'm kissing the gravel of the alleyway, my vintage Seger T getting rudely roughed up.

I curse and sit up and delicately pull some small rocks out of my right palm. What's another scrape or two in the scheme of things if I get to time travel?

I'm telling myself that, but I'm not leaping up to go catch the alien time traveler. I take my time. Assess the damage—something one must take more seriously as one gets older.

Okay, not "one," "me."

I must take this kind of thing more seriously because I am older. The body changes. It hurts more. It recovers slower. But then again, I have a body and my wife does not, so this is an observation not a complaint.

I take a deep breath and sigh. My wife doesn't have a body and that means I don't have a life.

I think I would have sat there for too long were it not for the sound of crying. It sounds like a girl, a soft sobbing coming from close by. It pulls at my heart and I'm not thinking about my aging body or my dead wife anymore.

I get up and move slowly forward and find a girl huddled into the narrow space between two aluminum trash cans, as if that will provide shelter for her. She's lanky and has light brown skin, dark hair, and brown eyes even more soulful than the dog's.

Her wavy black hair is pulled back into a ponytail and she is wearing a nightgown, dark blue with yellow stars.

My heart skips a beat (or ten). I know who it is. I know this story. It's one my wife told me after we had been a couple for a while about a mystical Seattle evening when this stranger came and told her she would be okay.

"Hi, Mia," I say, feeling my eyes fill with tears. "My name is Ash, and it's going to be all right."

She looks at me, her smooth brow furrowing and her turned-up little nose wrinkling. "Ash? That's a strange name."

"Well, I'm a strange person," I say. "I'm from the future and I'm here to tell you that what's going on inside between your parents, even though I know it's hard to see them fight and it's scary, is going to be okay."

"Future?" she asks.

I nod and sit down on the gravel in front of her. This girl is so young. She's not my Mia, not yet, but I can still see pieces of her. The mole on her left cheek. The way she bites her lower lip. Her insatiable curiosity.

"Yes. I've time traveled back from 2019," I say.

"How? Tell me." She is leaning, her troubles forgotten for the moment.

"A talking dog brought me here in her bone-shaped spaceship," I say.

She leans back, her forehead furrowing again. "I'm not stupid. I've seen the Mr. Peabody and Sherman cartoon, you know. I suppose your dog is white and wears glasses and likes to give history lessons."

I laugh because I hadn't realized how similar this all was to a cartoon that started around 1960. "No," I say. "My dog is named Angelica Huston and she's a tan and white corgi, and not one lecture so far. And as you can see, I'm not a boy named Sherman."

She shakes her head rapidly, her ponytail flopping back and forth. "No. You are an old man." She wrinkles her nose again.

Although Mia told me the story of this encounter from her perspective with fifteen years between, I don't worry about it. About if I'm saying the right thing or doing the right thing. I can't. I can only be who I am with this version of Mia.

And if Mia and I have done this before, can I really screw it up?

"I am old, so that makes me wise, right?" I ask.

She shrugs tentatively.

"You are a smart one, aren't you?" I say. "Age does not equal wisdom, but since I'm from the future, I know what's about to happen."

"You do?" She leans forward a bit.

I nod. "Right about now your parents have realized you are not in your room. They are starting to look for you. Soon they will get frantic. When you go in, they will act angry, but that's just because they are scared and they love you so much. And hidden behind them being scared, they will feel ashamed of their fighting and how it affects you."

She's biting her lip and nodding for me to continue.

"I know you feel like it's your fault," I say, "but your parents fighting is not about you. They are unhappy, that is all."

"Why can't they just love each other?" she asks.

And this one is hard for me to answer. My own marriage with the grown-up Mia was a good one. We fought, but not often. I never really doubted she was with me. "Sometimes people love each other but just can't get along," I say.

She nods slowly as if thinking about it.

"Look, a year from now everything will be very different, but everyone will be a lot happier," I say. "Can you trust me on that?"

She gives me another weak shrug and it's uncanny. It's one of the gestures she retained as an adult. It was always a signal that I hadn't gotten through to her.

"When you go in," I say, "your mom will see you first and she will say..." I take a moment, because this bit I have to get right. "She will say, 'Mia, you are my heart, and my heart can't take this.'"

Her brow furrows again. "That doesn't make any sense. How can I be her heart and her heart can't take it?"

There are shouts coming from the house on the other side of the fence. I can barely hear them, but Mia turns to look and then looks back at me, her eyes wide.

I get up and brush myself off. "Remember, Mia. If your mom says that, then you know I'm a time traveler and you know that in one year things will be different but a lot better."

I hear a muffled male voice calling out Mia's name.

She nods, getting up and peering timidly back towards her house. "Thank you, Mr. Ash," she says and then moves to the gate, opens it, and walks in without a second look.

I stand there listening. I can't hear the words, but I can hear the tone shift when they are reunited.

They've got a hard year in front of them, that is for sure.

"Ready?" Angelica Huston asks, panting next to me.

I'm not surprised that she is here. I don't know that anything will surprise me again.

I don't speak right away. I remember Mia telling me about

the encounter, about how the "old man" was too skinny and too old to be creepy. About how her mother said exactly what he said she would and that helped her through the year, through her parent's ugly divorce. She told me the man had a funny name but she couldn't remember what it was but that he really helped her.

I met Mia at a party some long-gone Seattle tech startup was having in 1996. I wouldn't have even gone and talked to her—she was way out of my league. Tall and hauntingly beautiful with straight hair just brushing her shoulders—she didn't like the waves and spent hours straightening it in those days. And she had these beautifully intelligent eyes. It was no surprise that I kept looking at her, but the surprise was she kept looking at me.

Believe me, this was not my experience with women. Ones that looked like Mia didn't ever stare at me. I remember going up to her and introducing myself.

"Have we met?" she asked. "You look so familiar."

In that misty alley in Seattle I squat down and look at the corgi. "If not for tonight," I say, "Mia and I would have never gotten together."

The dog licks my scraped hand and I hear her say, "You're smarter than the average ape, Ashton Bach. Ready for more?"

CHAPTER SIX

THE MIND IS A STRANGE THING... or, rather, *my* mind is a strange thing. I don't know about yours. I keep thinking about Mia and time travel and how Angelica Huston said her species was the only one with time travel.

And I think about this saying I've heard. I don't know if it's a saying or a thought experiment, but it goes something like this. If there was time travel, we would know it because the time travelers would be here. No matter how far in the future time travel was invented, they would be back in the past making their presence known.

But maybe they are and the time travelers are dogs, and it's our ape-centric view of the world that keeps us from seeing it. Maybe our ape-centric view of the world keeps us from seeing a lot of things. Important things.

"Only canines time travel?" I ask, following Angelica Huston through the quiet Seattle neighborhood. It's dark enough now that streetlights have come on and twinkle through the mist of the damp evening. I breathe deeply of the moist air, savoring the scent of flowers and growing things.

"The felines want it," she says in my head, "but that would be 'catastrophic.'"

She stops and looks at me, her head slightly cocked, and it takes me a moment. I'm still steeped in twelve-year-old Mia and this train of thought is largely a diversion. I chuckle when I get it. "Cat-astrophic. Good one. But why?"

She cocks her head to the other side like she's reevaluating my base intelligence level. "You ever heard of a seeing eye cat or a drug sniffing cat or a rescue cat?" she asks.

I shake my head, not sure where she is going. "No..."

"Dogs serve. Cats want to be served. Who do you want in control of the most powerful technology the universe has ever seen?"

With that she's trotting forward down the suburban sidewalk and I am walking fast to keep up with her.

My mind is thoroughly distracted by that. The most powerful technology in the universe is time travel. Because a small change can make a big difference. Which makes me wonder why the hell the universe's most powerful technology is being deployed to make sure Mia and I meet. She's dead. We didn't have any children. I haven't made any great contributions to the world.

"Why me?" I ask even before I've thought it through.

Angelica doesn't turn. "Why not you, Ashton Bach?"

"But... I... I'm nobody," I say. "I'm just a guy with a broken heart. Why does it matter if Mia and I meet? Why would you be using time travel for my benefit. Why?"

We're in front of the house whose yard the spaceship is

parked in. Angelica sits and nods towards the low wall that fronts the overgrown green yard, right in front of the for-sale sign. Apparently, time-traveling dogs have a database of vacant houses with large enough backyards to park their spaceships in.

I sit and those kind brown eyes are hard to look at.

"How do you feel after seeing her?" she asks.

I take a deep breath and sigh. "Well... it's complicated, but I... I feel..." A small smile creeps onto my face. "I'm so glad I got to meet her like that, to help her. It makes me understand her in a different way."

The dog nods. "And isn't that reason enough? Remember the whole dogs serve cats want to be served thing? Besides, there's time enough for—" She stops, her nose working and her pointed ears swiveling like a radar. And then she is barking with such intensity you would think the world is about to end. She tears around the side of the house towards the backyard barking even louder.

And given that canines control the universe's most powerful technology, maybe the world is about to end. I run after her and find her facing off with three cats in front of the silver bone-shaped spaceship, growling and her hackles raised.

The small yard is a tight fit for the spaceship with a couple of big maple trees leaning over it, the grass back here even longer than the front yard, a small covered patio with metal furniture attached to the back of the house.

At this juncture it is appropriate to say that I am not a cat person. I don't dislike them, but most cats seem to dislike me. I'm the one who will inevitably get scratched at almost any cat encounter.

While it's now clear to me that dogs are aliens, that is something I have always thought of cats. They just don't seem to be from around here. It's like they are all royalty banished to our primitive planet looking for a properly cushy place to live.

These three cats are hissing, their fur up and their backs arched. They are close to where the spaceship's hatch irises open. The one in the center is big and black and flanking it are two tabbies, and it kind of looks like Angelica Huston is out-gunned—well, out-clawed for sure. The black one is holding her attention while the tabbies move to flank her.

Well, I don't know Angelica Huston well, but she just gave me the kind of gift you can't repay. I grab a rake leaning against the fence and with a shout, I charge the big black cat.

Much to my surprise, it doesn't run away. It dodges my clumsy thrust of the rake, lets out a snarl, leaps, lands on my chest, and knocks me flat onto the damp weedy grass.

There I am with one of the biggest, fiercest cats I've ever seen sitting on my chest hissing, its yellow eyes making it look positively wild.

For a moment, things seem still and quiet. I don't hear Angelica's barking or the hissing of the tabbies. I hear my heart beating in my ear, but slowly. The cat raises its paw, its claws bared. Time is slowed, like it's all in slow motion. The cat's mouth opens, showing fangs and saliva, and I swear it is enjoying this.

The cat can't kill me. Not with one blow. It's not a panther or something. A dim part of me knows this, but the look in those eyes convinces me otherwise. Still in slow-motion, my heart thumps, the claws extend farther, and the paw swings for my face.

Yeah, my face is nothing to write home about. I'm sure when Mia and I started dating she didn't say to her girlfriends, "Oh, he is soooo dreamy." It was probably something more like, "He's kind and smart and that makes it okay that he has a huge nose and kind of a braying laugh."

But it's *my* face, you know? I see it every day in the mirror and I am not wanting to look in the mirror and see scarring that makes me look like some kind of Bond villain.

So what is an under-exercised, middle-aged geek supposed to do?

I scream. Like a girl. It's a shrill expulsion of fear and all the emotions of what I've just been through. It's full of the confused feelings I have about meeting twelve-year-old Mia. It's powered by the world-shattering realization that cats and dogs are aliens and time travel is real.

Time speeds back up and that cat freezes, its paw cocked back, claws fully extended.

I bought myself a moment with that scream. Less than a second. Sound descends again and I hear Angelica barking and the tabbies hissing and yowling.

I don't have time to think during that thin moment. I just react and swat at the cat like it's a mosquito or something.

Yes, that's right, ladies and gentlemen, Ashton Bach, while helping to defend the world's most powerful technology from a determined feline force, screams and swats.

My hand connects with the big cat as its paw comes crashing down towards me.

And yeah, I'm skinny and old-ish and don't do anything in

the way of upper body exercise and it's a big cat, but I still outweigh it by over a hundred pounds.

The swat works, the cat is unceremoniously removed from my chest and I collect a few painful scratches on my hand.

I surge up, brandishing the rake and the cat hisses and swats at it.

Angelica's barking is moving away as well as the hissing of the tabbies.

"That's right," I say, thrusting the rake. "It's just you and me now, kitty."

And then for the second time today I hear a voice in my head. But this one is hissing and deep. "This is not over, ape-man."

Well, that rattles my already very rattled brain. Both dogs and cats are telepathic? Why have they been holding out on us for so long? What does any of this mean in the larger scheme of things?

And that cat has an English accent too. Do all aliens learn to project the English language in London or something?

The cat is lunging, but I return to my senses in time and block it with the rake. "I won't be here long," I say a bit too smugly. "Time travel, you know."

The cat backs up a step and those yellow eyes of his just drill into me. "I smell you, ape-man. I know you. And my ancestors will know you too. You will know no peace from my kind, mark my words."

And then Angelica Huston is here and barking loud enough to wake the dead and the black cat is running off.

Well, at least I know why every cat on the planet seems to hate me.

CHAPTER SEVEN

AFTER THE BIG black cat is gone, I find myself sitting on the moist overgrown grass in the abandoned backyard staring at my reflection in the dog bone-shaped spaceship.

My mind is reeling. This rabbit hole is deep, way deep.

Angelica Huston licks my wounds and I feel unaccountably better. She is always doing that, like a dog will do, and every time she does, I feel better. Like there is something magical in her alien doggy saliva.

She licks her own wounds, too, but mine come first. She is a good dog.

I feel calm. I feel like the world is a good place and everything is going to work out. I don't really care about all the scrapes and scratches. I'm not so freaked out that I saw my apartment burn down, time traveled back thirty-five years, met the girl that would become my wife, and got in a fight with a big black cat that basically cursed me to have all his descendants know me and hate me.

"So... this is your first mission?" I ask, my mind wandering back to something Angelica Huston told me about getting promoted.

"Yes. I used to be on the catch-and-release team," she says in my head, her English accent taking on an unmistakable note of pride. "Reached the highest ranks there. Was chief human abductor for English speaking countries."

I smile and nod. That doggy saliva is good stuff. "Why did you abduct people?" I ask, rather innocently.

She pauses licking her wounds and stares at me, her adorable head cocked to the side. "We have been studying you apes for quite a long time now," she says. "My team was in charge of physical sample collection."

I nod again. I mean, my brain is processing this, correlating it with all the alien abductions stories that have been going around, but it doesn't bother me. The dogs are aliens. They've been studying us. Abducting us. Okay.

What is all of that against the backdrop of time travel and the canines from the dog star Sirius being in charge of it?

Soon we're back in the ship and I'm sitting on the soft grey surface of the bridge and Angelica Huston is on her pedestal. Seattle falls away below us, and when we can see the curvature of the Earth, there is that stutter, out-of-focus, stutter, in-focus thing going on and I feel sick and strange, smell something akin to burning plastic, and am so very fascinated by it all.

"When are we going?" I ask, after all this is not my first time jump and I know the question is always "when" not "where."

"1989," she says.

I rack my brain. 1989. George H. W. Bush was president. The Soviets were at the end of their mess in Afghanistan. Pan Am Flight 103 was blown up. The first Batman movie as well as the second Back to the Future movie came out. And Mia turned seventeen.

A pang of guilt hits me as I sit on the soft floor of the spaceship. There are things that could be done, things that would help the world, and I am thinking only of myself.

Maybe I should be more like a dog and focus on how I can serve.

And then it hits me. I have no idea what model of time travel we are operating on, so I have no idea what kind of actions might actually be of service.

Can the future be changed? Does each intervention result in a new parallel universe isolating your change to the new one? Is time fixed and are we just looping through time doing the things we have already done like I just did with Mia?

This is important stuff.

I mean, if you are going to time travel, you've got to know the science behind it and what the stakes are.

And, yeah, I get that science says time travel isn't possible, but I have evidence to the contrary.

Unless, of course, I'm still falling down the rabbit hole of my own psychotic break. Using the story Mia told me of the strange man that I reminded her of when we first met that helped her in 1984 and seemed to predict the future and inserting myself into it. But even if this is a momentary lapse of reason, there is no reason that my psychosis shouldn't make sense.

I babble to Angelica Huston asking her about how time

travel works and she turns from the pedestal, the grainy black-and-white view at the front of the bridge showing our descent back towards Earth.

"Don't be so binary, Ashton Bach," she says in my head.

I blink and rack my brain. "So... we do and don't create parallel universes when we change things and we can and can't change the past?"

She gives me a short bark. "Closer."

Closer? Closer to what? Me having a psychotic break? That is, provided I haven't already had one and then it would be a psychotic break within my psychotic break. Lovely.

But the calming effect of Angelica Huston's lick flows over me again and my thoughts become more orderly.

I just saw Mia and did something that had already affected my life. So, in this case, time travel has an effect, but since that effect had already happened, you are changing and not changing the timeline. At the same time. Cause and effect are not so linear anymore.

Yeah, that calming doggy saliva is good stuff. Maybe what this world needs more of is to be licked by a friendly dog so we can all calm the hell down.

And then I have to wonder that if something drastic happened on a time-travel journey, something that hadn't happened before, maybe that would cause the timeline to fork and a parallel timeline to be created.

The whole "many worlds" thing I always found to be rather exhausting. Saying that for every possible choice being made at every point, a new parallel universe is created just because of that choice just sounds bonkers to me. So many universes and no real choice.

It's not like I quite get what Angelica is getting at, but it feels much more reasonable.

I babble on some more about this as we descend toward the Earth and she barks again and says, "Closer."

And then I see that we are approaching Seattle again. The clouds are thick, but I can see them tattering around the west coast and Puget Sound, making it clear where we are going. To the east, the white tipped peaks of Mount Adams, Mount Rainier, and Mount Baker poke through the blanket of clouds like the spine of some enormous creature moving below, the sun heading towards the horizon casting it all into sharp relief even on the grainy black-and-white display.

We plunge into the clouds and all thoughts of time travel and parallel universes and feline foes are erased, and all I can think of is Mia.

CHAPTER EIGHT

IT'S dark and damp and I feel like a real creep.

The sun is well down and I'm freezing in my shorts and Seger concert T-shirt. The Seattle high school across the street is fairly typical of a suburban eighties high school, a bit sprawling and rather plainly built out of cinder blocks painted in green and black, undoubtedly the school's colors.

I'm squatting behind a hedge of yet another vacant house watching the comings and goings of the school's teenage students. They move in small clumps, their young voices echoing in the damp air. A few are alone but most of the groups are three or four.

They spill out of the school in small groups, done with some kind of extracurricular activity, some going to cars, others walking off.

It's that I'm the middle-aged guy spying on teenagers that makes me feel like a creep. I mean, what reasonable explanation is there for a man of my age to be squatting behind a hedge watching the school?

Angelica Huston dropped me off here and trotted off, not telling me what's going on or what I am supposed to do. She left me with an enigmatic, "You'll know, now buck up and be a good ape."

With my luck, I expect the cops to find me at any moment and throw me in jail.

And yes, I'm looking for Mia with her long limbs and wavy black hair. I want to see her, just a glimpse. Maybe that is all I'm here for, just a look at the love of my life at another age and then I can go.

I rack my brain, but I can't remember much about her high school years. She didn't talk about it, really. I knew she played the clarinet, so there was probably band practice, but beyond that, I have no idea.

"What. The. Hell."

I turn and there she is, Mia at seventeen. She's even taller and more gangly than at twelve, dressed in tight jeans and a blue sweater with a letterman's jacket over it.

Pimples decorate her face, and her brown eyes are wide.

She had been walking down the street and I had been so focused on the high school, I hadn't noticed her.

I am a geek, after all, not a spy, and I've had a hell of a day. I mean, technically speaking, this is my third day in my third different year, but it is still a single subjective day.

"Hi, Mia," I say, a sheepish grin on my face. It slips out, what else can I say? I was worried that the police would find me trying to catch a glimpse of my future wife, but it's her that finds me.

"How the hell do you know my name?" she asks, her hand going into her jeans pocket.

I slowly stand up and back up a few steps, my sandaled feet cold on the damp grass.

"What the hell are you doing here?" she asks, her hand coming out of her pocket holding a small cylinder.

And how am I supposed to answer that? I don't even know. I can't tell her that an alien time traveler dropped me off with no instructions and that time traveler is a telepathic dog who has taken the name of an American actress.

So, I once again do what any self-respecting geek would do in such a situation. I run.

Any thought of my "mission" here is gone. It's clear I'm not going to have a nice heartfelt conversation with her and that anything I could possibly say will just turn me into a bigger creep in her eyes.

At the same time I turn to run, she sprays. That was a can of pepper spray she pulled out of her pocket and she knows how to use it.

I was turning so I only got a little in my eyes. Just enough to make them feel like they are on fire and make them water like Niagara Falls.

So, I'm running, my eyes watering, but at least I can see, kind of. And the benefit of being an out-of-shape desk jockey and running as fast as I can is that I am soon warm... and have a hell of a stitch in my side.

I stop, leaning against a tree trying to catch my breath. I seriously need to add some aerobic exercise into my daily routine.

I ran up a side street away from the high school, but it is

still in view. Through the tears, I can see Mia staring in my direction, shaking her head, and then turning to step off the curb and walk across the street.

At the same time, there is a screeching of tires as an old Dodge Charger comes careening around the corner.

Wait. Not old. This is time travel and it's 1989, so the Charger isn't that old, it just looks old to me. Just like the houses.

The car is weaving down the street, heading towards Mia and the high school. I open my mouth to scream at her to watch out, but the car is past before I get the chance.

And then I do the math in my head. Our encounter was short, but I delayed her maybe fifteen seconds.

Those fifteen seconds just saved her life.

And my future.

And that's worth the embarrassment and the pepper spray in the eyes.

CHAPTER NINE

IT'S GOT to be the same cat. The vacant Seattle home has motion-sensor security lights and swaths of harsh bright light illuminate him. Big and black with yellow eyes, hissing with his back arched.

I know, I know, there are about a million black cats, how can this be the same one?

Well, it was sniffing at where the portal is in the dog bone-shaped spaceship, and when it turns and notices me, I can see the recognition in its feral yellow eyes.

The scratch on my hand the cat delivered five years earlier is still fresh, still burning.

"I don't want to fight," I say.

After the incident with Mia, I kept going. This time I had paid attention to where Angelica Huston parked the spaceship, and I came back alone to the vacant house and the backyard where the spaceship is.

I have no idea where the dog is or what she might be up to.

"Well I do," the cat says in my head with the same British accent I remember. He stalks a step forward and hisses at me.

Yup, that is that cat. It had been five years for it and it didn't look any older, in fact, it looked bigger and stronger.

So, I'll admit, I want to run, but then I think about the whole "most powerful technology in the universe" thing. About the feline desire to acquire it.

But then I think—and yes, I do have the tendency to over-think absolutely everything—that because of my own strange relationship with cats, which I finally understand, that maybe I was off. I know what Angelica Huston said, but I don't know if you can take a dog's word when it comes to cats, or vice versa for that matter.

"*When* do you want to go?" I ask and feel pretty proud asking a casual question in time-travel speak.

"None of your business, ape," he says, taking another step forward. Well that confirms that is what they are after.

Now, I haven't picked up the animal and examined its genitals, as is common—and quite rude—when wondering at the gender of a pet, but because of the deep rumble and size of this one, I have determined that the cat is a he.

He is stalking around me, getting behind me so I have a clear shot of getting to the ship. I glance around for a weapon, but there is nothing in this grassy backyard. A swing set on the other side of the spaceship and some nice overgrown flower beds against the wooden privacy fence, but no handy rakes or bats or rocks or anything.

He yowls and in a few moments three other cats join him. Two tabbies, probably the same from our encounter five years ago, and a big Siamese with haunting blue eyes.

They hiss and slowly close in on me and I have nowhere to go but to back up to the ship. Where is Angelica Huston?

"Nice kitties," I say, my voice almost breaking.

I have a lifetime of getting scratched by cats for no reason —well, there is a reason, but I just found out—and now I have four determined aliens with claws and I know that this is not going to end well.

They are closing in. I am backing up and bump into the cool, smooth metal of the spaceship, nowhere left to go. The black cat out half a step in front of its companions, determined to strike the first blow.

This is going to get bloody and this is going to get painful, so I do the same damn thing I did in 1984. I scream. At the top of my lungs.

It isn't manly. It isn't dignified. But, apparently, my wimp scream is not enjoyed by cats. They back up a step. I see an opening and I run.

I feel a scratch at my ankle but otherwise get out of the yard unscathed. But I'm mad. I had tried to be reasonable. I had tried to have a discussion, and they had insisted on violence.

I am huffing on the sidewalk two houses down thinking this through. They hadn't followed, and I notice a hose setup on the side of the yard the spaceship is in.

I sneak back. I slowly turn on the hose, cringing at the squeak, and then peer around the corner and see the four cats still sniffing around where the portal opens into the ship.

With great pleasure, I leap out and hose all four of those cats down.

They hiss. They screech. They are quickly soaked and then they are quickly gone.

"Well done, Ashton Bach," Angelica Huston says in my head as she trots into the backyard. "I was wondering how you would handle them."

I'm sputtering incoherent syllables. She knew. She left me to face them alone. She put me in that terrible situation with the seventeen-year-old Mia instead of letting me just delay her in a less embarrassing way.

"You coming?" she calls from the spaceship portal. "Or do you want to stay in this time?"

CHAPTER TEN

IF THIS WERE A MOVIE, now would be the time for a montage. The one in which Angelica Huston and I go up into the atmosphere in her spaceship until the curve of the Earth is visible and there is the shudder, out-of-focus, shudder, in-focus thing as we change times. I smell that burning plastic smell and I feel sick and my skin is hot and itchy and then we are back in Seattle where we deal with an annoying, and growing, band of cats and I have odd encounters either directly with Mia or tangential to Mia.

It's all about her. Every single jump. I get to see a different version of her, every single time.

I'm there to stop her tripping and falling down the stairs her first day in college.

I'm there to keep her from walking out into a crosswalk and getting creamed by a drunk driver running a red light.

I'm there to say "You're crazy if you don't offer her the

job" to the woman that hires her right out of college after their interview over coffee.

I'm there to see what she looks like after she cuts her beautiful long hair off after a bad breakup.

I'm there to see her brief college hippy phase and her post-college yuppie phase too.

This montage would be interspersed with cat encounters that involve me facing a growing band of cats led by that big black one.

You would also see me acquiring some clothing at a secondhand store and start having my encounters with Mia in disguise. The prize of this being a long black duster similar to what Neo wore in *The Matrix*.

You would also see me find and carry several water pistols and care for them like many people care for real guns. You would see me deploy them repeatedly in defense of the bone-shaped canine spaceship. You would see the pistols working at first, but after a few encounters the number of cats would become too much and you would watch me buy and deploy a long water blaster rifle that I carry slung under that glorious duster.

I'm not the time-travel neophyte I was for those few trips. I walk with confidence and I carry a lot of water guns.

And when thinking about music, the whole thing would likely be backed by The Police's 1983 hit "Every Breath You Take."

Because weirdly, and maybe creepily, I was there watching and taking care of Mia. Time after time.

Oh, wait. Let's switch that backing track to Cyndi Lauper's 1983 hit "Time after Time." Much better.

So, jump after jump, I am there with Mia providing the guardian angel nudges in her young life interspersed with cat battles involving squirt guns while I'm rocking a black duster all to the earnest sounds of Lauper's "Time after Time."

After eight total jumps, we're back in the ship and I am exhausted. I look cool in my shades and duster, but the constant pace is getting to me.

"Can we take a break?" I ask with a yawn. Angelica Huston has hopped onto the little control pedestal and is about to put her paws in. "And maybe we should get some food. This is time travel, isn't there time enough for food and rest?"

She turns, her head tilting and her radar ears pointing right at me, and she just stares, panting. Our last cat battle was vigorous, but now that I am fully clothed, I escaped without any new scratches.

"But Mia needs you," she says in my head.

"You're kidding, right?" I ask. "Time travel. We go somewhere, fill our bellies, take a shower, sleep for twelve hours and we'll still be back in time."

The corgi turns from me and puts her paws into the pedestal's holes and the front display comes to life. It's not a grainy black-and-white view of the Earth this time, but a twisting 3D view of bright lines dancing through a dark void with an odd script written on them.

The view is black and white still and grainy still, but as Angelica Huston stands there, we zoom out and see how these lines are really just threads in a much larger tapestry and then we zoom in and are looking at a single thread, much thicker and brighter, and how it interacts with all the threads around it.

That has to be Mia.

And there is another thread that comes in from far away and keeps crossing her thread at a sharp angle.

That must be me.

It's a tangle and rather hard to discern much, but soon I see a third thread that must be Angelica Huston and a tangle of other threads that must be our cat nemesis and his gang.

All these lines weave and interact diving in and out of proximity with each other in ways that even look complicated on this display. I have to imagine that this being just a representation of how we interact through time that the reality is much more complicated.

And what is this technology that can track this? Exactly how sophisticated are these canine aliens? Now I am really starting to appreciate that "most powerful technology in the universe" thing.

This is with me just barely grasping what I am seeing.

The lines, timelines I guess, are bright until they hit an invisible marker that is slowly moving and then they turn dull and ghostly for a bit and then they diffuse into incoherent vapor. That must be the line of "now" as time slips by. The tangle of lines that is the cats had moved away but are moving back closer to us. The line of Mia is barely in the view; her line is interacting with other lines now.

"We have to go now," Angelica says.

And the display shifts and I see the Earth falling below us. I miss the lines, the timelines. There was something lulling and comforting about them.

"One more stop and we'll be done," Angelica says. "Buck

up, my ape friend. I'll have you home soon and you can sleep all you like."

I lie down on the soft floor of the ship and take a little cat nap while she takes us up, while we jump in time, and while she takes us back down.

CHAPTER ELEVEN

ANY TIME-TRAVEL STORY you watch or read will warn you about meeting a past version of yourself. You might tell yourself something you shouldn't know. You might hurt yourself or keep yourself from doing what you should have done.

What they don't tell you about is the utter horror you might experience on seeing your past-self.

Remember that fancy startup party where I told you I met Mia? Well, I'm there in my black duster and I can see the dork that is the twenty-something me standing alone in a corner nursing a rum and Coke.

It's 1996 and my past-self is wearing a sweater vest, for God's sake. A plaid sweater vest in black and green!

I have no recollection of this. Zero. I mean, I am no fashionista, but a sweater vest? How did I get Mia's attention in the first place? Was that the reason she kept looking at me? I desperately want to go up to myself, rip that damn sweater vest off, and kick myself in the ass.

Not to mention the shaggy brown hair that slumps into my face. That, at least, I understand. I was growing my hair out, feeling confident enough in my job to know that no one really cares what the geek looks like as long as the code gets written.

But that middle stage is just terrible. It's like a furry brown helmet squatting on my head.

The party's location is a bar in a renovated industrial loft with aged brick walls, exposed ventilation, lots of little round tables, and a long wooden bar. The lights are soft and the music is a bit loud and way too nineties for me with milling young people that will soon be known as hipsters in their skinny jeans and beanies, expensive drinks in their hands.

And then I see Mia and... well, I can hardly see anything else. She's tall and slim, her black hair straightened and grown out enough to hang to her shoulders. She has a shy smile on her face that lifts up the mole on her left cheek. She's wearing a simple black sleeveless dress with a short skirt and a fit that accentuates her graceful form and her long limbs. She has a silver clutch in her hand.

She walks in with a dark-haired man that I know is a friend from college and looks around with a smile. She merges into the sea of people with a confidence I could never manage, saying hello, chatting, smiling, eyes following her when she moves on.

My younger self stays put with that rum and Coke, having several conversations with some people who float by. It looks like the rum and those conversations are relaxing the younger me.

Not that I look any better relaxed in that damn sweater.

And then I remember. The sweater was a gift from my mother and I had worn it knowing there would be pictures taken and then I could show her I wore it and she would be so happy.

A nice thought but a terrible look.

And this is the guy that currently lives in shorts, T-shirts, and sandals most of the time speaking. It's not like I know what good fashion is, but I know that a sweater vest is never in fashion.

Angelica Huston is waiting outside. She sent me in with very specific instructions. At 9:03 PM I am to walk over to my younger self, deliver my line, and then leave.

And then my life will be on track—again? For the first time?—and Mia and I will fall in love and...

Well, that is where it gets sticky. What about that "and"? *And* we will have a nice life together, *and* Mia will end up with pancreatic cancer. *And* she will have a very difficult end. *And* I will be by her side for it all. *And* end up a husk of who I once was.

As I watch Mia circulate effortlessly and I watch my awkward younger self in his sweater vest, I have to wonder about it all. What if I don't deliver my line? What if Mia and I never get together? Surely, I would meet someone else. Maybe someone who didn't die tragically young.

Or maybe I should talk to Mia, warn her of the coming cancer diagnosis, maybe if she sought treatments at first symptom, the back pain and fatigue, maybe she could have beaten it, could have survived longer.

The other things I did as Mia's time-traveling guardian angel were clear and easy. Comfort her while her parents argued. Stopping her from getting run over by a car, several times. Helping her get a job. All of that was clearly worth doing. This... I just don't know.

And I had too much time to think. The hipster/yuppies swirl around me, most of them giving a wide berth to the tall old guy in dark shades and a long duster. Little do they know that in three years when *The Matrix* comes out, this will be as cool as you can get.

And then it is 8:30 PM and Mia has settled at the bar with a group of friends and keeps looking at my younger self.

Of course she is. Me, the twenty-three-years older version of that sweater-vested geek has been in and out of her life since she was twelve. A few times quite recognizably. The difference in ages and the long hair will keep her from putting it together, but the recognition is clearly there.

And then I'm freaking out about how this time travel works where you apparently can and can't change the time-line and you do and don't create new parallel universes.

If I don't do my part, will I disappear, fork the timeline, cause all of reality to implode because of the paradox? Okay, that last one is silly, but you get the picture. My mind is running amok.

And then a woman is standing in front of me, a smile playing on her red lips. She is tall, almost six feet, with short blond hair, light blue eyes, and generous curves dressed simply in black jeans and a black sweater with a rain jacket draped over her arm. "Let's go, Bach," she says. "You know you can't do this."

My jaw drops and just hangs there. If you were looking at us, you'd figure I'm a lonely weirdo who never gets this kind of attention. But I'm really just trying to figure out how she knows who I am.

"What... I... Who...?" I stammer.

She smiles, showing off white teeth and rather pronounced canines. Like, not a vampire, but noticeable.

"You say hello," she whispers, nodding at Mia and moving so her side is pressed to mine, "you say goodbye." Her movements are graceful, sinuous even, like she's a dancer or something. She has enough perfume on for me to smell it and it's almost too strong, the floral note filling up my nose and chasing away the smell of alcohol and too many bodies.

I take a deep breath and get my brain engaged. She knows what I am doing here, so that means that either Angelica Huston sent her or...

"Let me guess," I say, trying to sound as cool as I look. "You are a *cat* person."

She laughs—it's a bright sound and fills my ears. "You're not as dumb as he said you'd be."

He being the big black cat with yellow eyes that keeps trying to get into Angelica Huston's time-traveling spaceship.

And then she stands on her tiptoes and whispers in my ear, her breath warm. "Let's get out of here. I'll make it worth your while. I promise."

A shiver runs down my spine as my body responds to her presence and her offer. It has been a long time for me. Since Mia got really sick. I may be over fifty, but I am still quite human. And she is quite lovely.

But I'm not that shy geek in the sweater vest anymore. I know what a real relationship feels like and I know the power of love beyond attraction that lifts up and makes passion all the better.

And besides, Mia is here, young and beautiful and so full of life. My body may respond to this cat person, but the rest of me does not.

The doubts I had about doing my part here, ensuring that my younger self ends up talking to Mia, evaporate. Time travel may be the most powerful technology in the universe, but love is the most powerful force. Mia and I had love. Not long enough, true, but it would never have been long enough, even if we lived to be old and wrinkled and died together in our sleep.

"While I appreciate the offer," I say. "I'm good right here."

I feel something hard press to my side. My heart leaps and adrenaline flows through my system. The cat person has a gun hidden under the raincoat on her arm.

"I'm afraid I have to insist," she says.

I feel like such a fool. Thinking I'm Neo-cool in my black duster, but all I have hidden are squirt guns which work fairly well in chasing off cats but are nothing compared to a real gun.

Not that I would know how to shoot a gun in real life. Sure, I've done it so many times in video games, but that's not like dealing with a real weapon and real bullets and real blood.

"Now," she says, her voice still sweet, shoving the gun painfully into my ribs. "We go right now, and I'll leave your beloved Mia alone. Delay one more second and I'll come back and shoot her after I deal with you."

I've seen enough movies to know that time travel often

gets tricky, that the heroes must defend time itself from being tampered with, that the stakes are always sky high.

But those are movies and they don't involve intelligent alien canines and felines. What once was a fun, if exhausting, jaunt has turned into something different. Something serious.

I don't argue. I walk out the door with the cat person behind me.

CHAPTER TWELVE

"WHY ARE YOU DOING THIS?" I ask. She has been marching me towards where the spaceship is hidden in the back of another vacant house just a few minutes' walk from the bar.

The clouds have cleared and a few stars are bright enough to outshine the lights of the city. The sidewalks are wet from the recent rains and the cars make a hissing sound as they pass by on the wet road. The city smells fresh and alive—this was my favorite time when I lived here.

She doesn't answer. She hasn't spoken more than necessary. As I think about it, I guess I shouldn't be surprised that the cats recruited a human. Angelica Huston recruited me with the "come with me if you want to live" line and saving my life.

We quickly walk from the industrial neighborhood in the midst of gentrification to an older neighborhood with modest houses built of brick.

In the small backyard, I see Angelica Huston, her paw held up as if injured. She's got her back to the silver bone-shaped spaceship, blood on her face, surrounded by a dozen cats.

"Any luck?" the woman asks when we are all in the yard.

The yellow-eyed big black cat turns slowly. He is clearly old now, his fur matted down but his yellow eyes still bright. He swishes his tail staring at the woman.

"That's too bad," she says.

Well, that tells me something about these aliens and their telepathic communication. It is, or can be, just person to person.

"You okay, Angelica?" I ask.

"Run, Ashton Bach," she says in my head, her own head hanging down, dejected. Even in defeat, her tone has that British sense of dignity. "I have triggered the self-destruct sequence. The felines must never capture our technology. It looks like I just don't have what it takes to make it in this time-travel business."

Running, well, I'm good at that, but the woman still has her gun pointed at my chest and I have to figure that dying in an explosion is a better way to go than a bullet in the back. And besides, can I abandon Angelica Huston, the dog person that I am?

And then my geek brain goes into high gear asking questions like, what would Neo do? What would Schwarzenegger's benevolent T-800 do? What would Marty McFly do?

Now that last one is way more my speed. In *Back to the Future*, Marty would grab a hoverboard and outwit the bad guys, but no one had a gun in that movie.

And all I've got are squirt guns.

"Seriously?" the woman asks, taking a step forward, continuing her conversation with the black cat. "But you promised this would work. That I would get to go back to..."

A squirt gun is still a gun. It doesn't deliver a bullet to tear through flesh and blood, but it does deliver a stream of water and I've gotten to be pretty accurate and pretty quick on the draw. And these squirt guns have been doctored a bit. The cats had come to care about them less so I added some cayenne pepper to the batch that is on me.

So in what I like to think is a nearly perfect merging of Neo and Marty McFly, I sweep back my duster, pull the two large, black squirt guns holstered there, and fire.

The woman dressed in black isn't expecting me to do anything but stand there and cower like a big ole geek. Her mistake.

And it may be only water with a little cayenne in my guns, but I hit her square in the face and refine my aim so my two streams of water hit directly in her eyes.

Squirt guns with their relatively slow trajectory and issues with wind and the like are actually tricky to use. The farther away you are the more disorganized the water streams are. I chose the pistols because, while they don't have a lot of capacity, they are accurate to about twenty feet.

She curses, cries out in pain, closes her eyes, and shields her face with her arms. The cayenne is working. It may not be pepper spray, but it's not just water anymore.

I drop the empty guns, run two steps, and tackle her. She drops her real gun and goes down. We wrestle briefly and soon she is on top of me and she punches me in the face.

Okay, well, I guess I should have seen that coming. Clearly this cat person does some sort of upper body exercise. I'm not much taller than her and certainly not as strong as she is.

At the same time the squirting, wrestling, punching is going on, I hear hissing and barking from the direction of Angelica Huston and the cats. The barking is at first sharp and defiant, but quickly becomes a yelp. She doesn't stand a chance with that many cats.

The blond woman is groping around for her gun when I get up, just a little bit dizzy, tasting blood and my mouth hurting like hell. Did she loosen a tooth?

She can't see very well, which has delayed her, but I don't know if it will be enough. She's a couple of steps away from me, her hand almost to the sleek black gun.

The duster and the Neo ethic serves me, and I pull two more weapons from under my duster. These are sixteen-ounce spray bottles with way more capacity than a squirt gun, and fancy ones at that. The bottle is made out of stainless steel and contains my water/cayenne mix. They are not as accurate as the squirt guns I started with but have a lot more firepower.

I step towards the cat woman and start squirting into the mass of undulating fur, hitting a few cats.

The woman has found her gun and is standing up. Her eyes are red-rimmed and she appears to be having trouble focusing.

I redirect my stream to her face as I close in and don't slow down. I barrel into her and knock her over and find myself in the middle of a roiling mess of cats and dog.

Angelica Huston's jaw is snapping, the cats are howling,

their claws tearing at anything they can find. I'm squirting and yelling and kicking, my long duster serving to parry most of the swiping claws.

It's chaos, glorious chaos. This is no video game, and the stakes are sky high, the most powerful technology in the universe falling into the wrong paws, but that doesn't mean it can't be fun, right?

Angelica and I are taking hits but we are making progress. It's ten cats on us and then six and then five.

At that point we are side by side, our backs against the spaceship and my spray bottles run dry.

The five cats stop, ringed around us with the old black cat in the middle and the cat woman steps forward. Her eyes are red and watering, but she looks like she's recovered from the spray and levels her gun at me.

"Open the ship or your pet human dies," she says.

"Don't do it," I say to the corgi.

"Well, to tell you the truth, Ashton Bach, I wasn't going to," Angelica says in my head with more than a dash of British derision.

"Really?" I ask. Yeah, not my finest moment there after all that Neo-inspired spraying of cats and disabling of a human.

The corgi looks at me, so much empathy in those big brown eyes. "No way, bub," she says. "We are talking about the most powerful technology in the universe. You and I don't really matter compared to that."

I nod and sigh. And then I remember Mia and my sweater-vested self still sitting in the bar. I need to get back there. I need to make sure I meet her. Love is the most powerful force in the universe and that younger me needs to experience it, and all the heartbreak that will eventually come after it.

There has to be a way.

I feel the plastic water cannon hung inside my duster bang against my hip and I have a plan. A bad plan. A sure to fail plan. But if we are going to die, why not?

I sink to my knees in defeat and turn to the spaceship, my shoulders hunched. "No!" I cry out.

I'm no actor and I need to cry, how am I going to do that? My hands are wet with cayenne water so I wipe my eyes, feel the burn and soon my shoulders are heaving and I am crying. For Mia. For my soon to be death. For my stupid, desperate plan.

"I am so sorry, Ashton Bach," Angelica says in my head as she nuzzles against my side. "This is most definitely not the result I was expecting. Even an ape like you deserves better than this."

"Distraction," I hiss in between sobs. "Do something."

I hear restrained British laughter in my head and then she turns and starts howling.

Now this is not some domesticated howl of a well-cared for pet—this is the lonesome howl of a being about to lose everything they care about, about to lose their life. It pulls at my heart and it strengthens my resolve.

The woman is shouting at Angelica to stop. The cats are yowling. I unclip the water cannon, hold it to my chest, roll on my back and fire. Right into the woman's eyes.

This thing is just a long tube with a plunger you press down. It doesn't have much life, but it does have quite the powerful stream.

The woman sees my movement and shoots her gun just as I fire the water cannon.

The bullet, being faster than the stream of water, lands first, thunking into the spaceship where my head had just been.

The cayenne laden stream hits next, finding its mark and filling her eyes up. She screams, drops the gun, her hands going to her face.

At the same time, the corgi turns into a whirling dervish of lunging, snapping jaws, and wolf-level growling. Cats screech. Fur flies. And I make a mental note to never piss off Angelica Huston.

I get up and the woman is once again feeling around for her gun, but I get to it first. I don't like the feel of it, all black and heavy and full of death. Squirt guns are, honestly, much more my speed, and I say that without any shame.

"What did he promise you?" I ask after backing up a few paces from the woman. Angelica's bark and the hiss of the cats are getting farther away as she chases the rest of them off.

The cat woman looks up at me and she is a pitiful sight, her face red, her eyes swollen, and snot leaking from her nose. She looks older than she did in the bar. She's in great shape, clearly with her being a lot stronger than me, but she's got to be in her mid-forties, that short blond hair chemically enhanced.

"My dad," she says. "He promised to let me see my dad one more time before he dies."

I feel for her. I would give just about anything to see Mia again, to have a few more moments with her even though I've just been in and out of her young life. What I really want is to see her again when she knows who I am and what we mean to each other. I want to tell her that I love her one last time.

And then I remember Mia and I look at my watch. 8:59 PM. I have four minutes to go deliver my line.

I holster the real gun and say, "Stay here. Tell Angelica Huston when she comes back. Maybe we can help you."

"What?" she asks, her red face full of surprise. "You would.... Wait. Who the hell is Angelica Huston? Do you mean the actress from the Addams Family movies?"

"No!" I shout as I run away. "I mean the dog! And don't mention that movie."

CHAPTER THIRTEEN

AS I STRIDE across the crowded bar with its clusters of hipsters and geeks with loud music playing and my heart beating even louder, I try to look cool but my breath is labored and my body sweaty and my mouth hurting from being punched and my new scratches bleeding from the fight with the cats and my eyes still burning from the little bit of cayenne water I got in it.

Kinda hard to look cool with all that going on.

As I stride across the bar, I remember this moment from twenty-three years ago, standing in the corner alone, my second rum and Coke just about gone, seeing the old homeless guy stride toward me. He's in a long dirty coat and has ripped jeans and reeks of sweat and spicy food. He's wearing sunglasses and his hair is kind of in a ponytail, but many strands are pulled out and haloing his face. I remember thinking the homeless guy must have really liked Corey Hart and his "Sunglasses at Night" song.

I am remembering the moment from my younger self's point of view and living it from the other end for the first time. It's this strange feedback loop that is quite disorienting.

But my line is simple and it echoes in my memory as I say it to my younger self. I nod toward Mia at the bar who is, thankfully, not looking at us right now. "She's been watching you all night," I say. "You'll regret it forever if you don't at least go introduce yourself."

My sweater-vested younger self had noticed Mia, of course. With that beautiful black hair, those long graceful limbs, those soulful brown eyes, how could I not? I had wanted to do something but lacked the courage. That old homeless guy had pushed me over the edge.

I walk away quickly and glance back before I leave the bar and see my younger self introducing himself to Mia. The spark is obvious, despite the damn sweater vest. I know that spark will turn into the flame of love and that love will outlive Mia's biology.

I know that because I still love her and I would not trade my time with her for anything in this world.

CHAPTER FOURTEEN

HER NAME IS JESSICA COLE, the cat person, that is, and she wants to say goodbye to her father.

I dumped the real gun into a trash can on the way back, and while I know she is physically stronger, the spaceship needs four paws to operate, so I think we are okay.

The battle is over. My future with Mia secured. We're in the vacant backyard which smells vaguely of cayenne and shows signs of the battle with areas of the overlong grass stomped and crushed.

Jessica is apologetic and kind now that she thinks we can get her what she wants, but Angelica has a different thought.

"Tell her to come back here in one week, unarmed," she says in my head. I relay the message wondering why Angelica doesn't do it herself. Is this telepathic ability limited in some way, or is the dog just mad?

I can see the wheels turning behind Jessica's bloodshot blue eyes. She's calculating, considering her options, and then her shoulders fall. "Thank you," she says meekly and walks away.

I look at the corgi, her radar ears rotating in the direction of the receding woman. "What was that all about?" I ask.

Angelica tilts her head, her big brown eyes studying me, evaluating me. "Just buying some time." She turns and the spaceship irises smoothly open and she jumps in. "I told you I'd get you back in time, so let's get to it, eh?"

A short trip up, a nauseating time jump, and a short trip down and we are back in Phoenix, Arizona, and I'm trotting after a corgi, overdressed for the desert in my Neo outfit.

It looks like 2019 to me, but I could be wrong. The sprawl of Phoenix has looked this way for a long time. Angelica isn't saying much.

We wind through the residential neighborhood and end up out in front of my apartment complex, except there is no fire, my apartment whole and undamaged.

"Stand here," Angelica says, sitting on the grass at the edge of the sidewalk near the busy street with two lanes of traffic buzzing in each direction.

"Why?" I ask.

"Because it is important, Ashton Bach," she says.

I shrug and stand there next to the corgi, sweating in the duster and the ripped jeans, grateful for the sunglasses.

"Why don't you call me Ash," I say, finally feeling confident enough after defending the world's most powerful technology against a determined pack of cats and an armed cat person to ask for the nickname I want.

"Very well, Ash," she says. "You may call me Angelica Huston."

I smile. At least I could get a dog to use my preferred nickname, almost forty years later. Well, not a dog, really. A technologically advanced, telepathic alien. Now that is something. And Ash makes me sound tougher than I really am. As if the corgi is the nice one of the two of us and I am the badass. That's not true, of course. I played my part, but Angelica is the one with the time-traveling spaceship and the plan.

It's been a hell of a subjective day... or two ... or three? I have no idea how long it's been in terms of hours since the corgi saved my life, but I do know I haven't eaten in that long. A wave of dizziness hits me now that all the craziness is over and I sway there on the sidewalk next to the busy street.

I really need to eat. I really need to sleep. The traffic is mesmerizing and time slips by me and I have no idea how long I've been there.

Another wave of dizziness hits me and I step off the curb and jump back when the blaring of a horn nearly scares me to death.

There is the screeching of brakes, more horns, and then a loud clang as an old red pickup truck jumps the curb right in front of me and goes barreling towards my apartment building.

As the truck bounces over the grass going right towards my office window, I realize something. That homeless guy I had seen out my windows was me.

I had caused the accident that Angelica Huston used to "save" my life and pull me into all of this. I *am* causing that accident.

I stumble back and trip and fall heavily on the rough

desert grass on the other side of the sidewalk, the corgi nowhere to be seen.

The truck slams into my apartment, crashing through the window and into my office. I just stare. I can't look away. Moments later I see myself in shorts and a Bob Seger concert T-shirt on the grass in front of the building, the past Angelica Huston with me.

Now I'm really dizzy, but I lever myself up and walk in the other direction. I don't want the police talking to two versions of myself, and I can't let my past-self see me up close.

I glance back and see myself looking at the dog and then looking back at the apartment building, the scent of smoke just reaching me. I know I'll do the right thing and warn my neighbors and still have the adventure of a lifetime.

And then I smile. The second time Angelica Huston used her line on me she said, "Come with me if you want to live *again*." And I do feel like I am living, really living, for the first time in years.

See, I told you it would get weird. Time travel is real, but it's the canines not the apes that have control of the technology. Dogs are aliens and so are cats and both are telepathic—or at least some are. And sometimes squirt guns are better than real guns.

Sure, that time-traveling dog seemed to have used me, but I got to know my beloved Mia in ways I never imagined. She may be gone, but my love for her is not.

Wait. This is time travel we are talking about. Mia is back there alive and well in the past, if I can just find Angelica Huston and get her to take me back in time.

PART TWO

THE TANGLED TAPESTRY OF TIME

CHAPTER FIFTEEN

AFTER SLEEP and some time to recover, I'm pretty convinced I made it all up. A fevered dream caused by the trauma of that pickup crashing through the wall of my home office. And the lingering trauma of Mia's death and me being widowed and alone and middle aged.

Mix in Mia thinking I looked familiar when we met with her story of a strange man that claimed to have time traveled with a dog, add to that that I just happen to resemble the old smelly guy that encouraged me to introduce myself to Mia at that bar, and then keep in mind my own obsessive consumption of science fiction since I was a kid, and there you have it.

Dogs aren't aliens.

Dogs aren't telepathic.

Dogs aren't the keepers of the most powerful technology in the universe: time travel.

Cats also aren't aliens and trying to wrest the most powerful technology in the universe from the dogs.

And there's not a time-traveling corgi running around speaking in people's head with an elegant English accent who has taken on the name of her favorite actress, Angelica Huston.

See. When I say it like that it does sound like a fevered dream, something Buckaroo Banzai might prattle on about, except for the fact that idea is too tame for him.

Except the part about cats. Most everyone I know thinks cats are aliens, and not just the dog people, but some of the cat people too. Cats are clearly not like us, acting more like displaced royalty wanting us apes to wait on them hand and paw.

"Honey," my mother calls from downstairs. "Are you coming?"

Yes. I am fifty years old and living with my parents. A truck did crash into my apartment, that part is real, for sure.

"Ashton," mom calls again. "Your eggs are getting cold."

My room is surprisingly neat. For me. Which is to say that the bed is unmade and some of my clothes strewn about. And my new laptop is open on the narrow wooden desk.

After that truck crashed into my apartment, I lost every-thing. Well... "everything" possession-wise except for my beloved Bob Seger concert T-shirt which is safely tucked into a drawer so I don't lose every physical connection I have with my past.

I really lost "everything" when Mia died. And, yes, that sounds dramatic and isn't literally true, but it is the way it felt. Actually, it still feels that way.

I feel slightly guilty letting my room be even this messy with my mother's rather compulsive fastidious streak, but it doesn't matter. My parents aren't great with stairs anymore and the second floor is pretty much all mine.

The whole adventure with Angelica Huston and traveling back in time, seeing Mia and basically being her guardian angel, and battling the cats trying to take Angelica's silver bone-shaped time-traveling spaceship would seem like a fevered dream except for the scratches from the cats. And the swollen lip from Jessica Cole. And the scraped knee and hand from being an out of shape klutz.

The knee, hand, and the swollen lip I could blame on the truck crashing into my apartment, but not the scratches.

I look at my hand and my forearm at the long thin scratches, scabbed up with angry red skin on either side. Either some cats got to me or I found some raspberry bushes to mess with in Phoenix, Arizona.

And then there's the other physical evidence of what happened. I walk over to the closet, which is the tacky mirrored variety, slide open the door, and look at the long black duster hanging there. The same kind Neo wore in the *Matrix*, the pockets jammed with the squirt guns I used to fight the cats with.

This is also hard to dismiss as a fevered dream, unless I was wandering around Phoenix buying this stuff and pretending to save Mia and defend the most powerful technology in the universe from a pack of determined cats.

I came to my parents' house after whatever happened (either time-traveling adventures or just watching my apartment building burn to the ground) and slept for sixteen hours.

I bought a new laptop yesterday, checked in on my client and pretended that none of it had happened.

Maybe it was all my mind desperately looking for closure. Combined with a psychotic break that included buying some weird stuff and getting scratched up. I mean, it sounds like that, doesn't it?

"Ashton Bach!" my father yells. "It's now or never on breakfast."

That just makes me feel like a teenager not a middle-aged widower. It's what would have happened when I was a teenager. My mom would try and if I wasn't responsive, it would be turned over to my father who would just get loud.

When I was a kid, I asked my friends to call me Ash, and when I was a teenager, I asked my parents to. But none of them would. Not until the time-traveling telepathic dog, Angelica Huston, agreed to after our adventures.

"Ashton" just seems too long and formal to me, but "Ash" sounds cool.

The dog called me Ash. At least in my mind.

"I'm coming, Dad!" I yell back.

I close the closet door and take one last look at the scratches. They have to be from cats, don't they? This couldn't have been some kind of fevered dream or bad trip, could it have? I couldn't have had some kind of psychotic break watching all my possessions burn and done this to myself, could I?

I think the problem with a psychotic break is that, well, you have to "break" for one to happen. So how the hell am I to know, stuck in my own head, if it was real or it was a psychotic break?

With a sigh, I turn to go, but then I catch my reflection in the mirror and look at my mouth. The right side is swollen from where I was punched. Her name is Jessica Cole and she was recruited by the cats and tried to help them take Angelica's ship away. We fought, she got the better of me seeing how she is not a middle-aged geek with little to no upper-body strength, and punched me in the face.

"Jessica," I mumble, my mouth sore, the small bruise edging towards purple, my words slightly slurred from the remnants of the swelling.

We had been back in 1996, and after it was all over and the cats were routed and we were victorious, Angelica Huston had me tell her to come back in a week. The cats had promised that if they got the ship away from Angelica, they would take Jessica back to see her father one last time before he died.

"Jessica," I say, smiling even though it hurts some. I have a name. I know what she looked like twenty-three years ago. If I can find Jessica Cole, I can find out if this was a fevered dream / psychotic break or if time travel is real and dogs are telepathic.

And if I can find Angelica Huston and her silver dog-bone-shaped spaceship, maybe I can talk her into taking me back to see Mia one last time. Not when she is young and doesn't know me, but when she is sick and knows the end is coming. Maybe I can say goodbye to her one last time. Tell her that I love her, one more time.

Or maybe a couple of more times.

My father calls up again, but I ignore him and grab my laptop. I am a bit slinger for hire, after all. If there is a Jessica Cole, I can find her.

CHAPTER SIXTEEN

JESSICA COLE still looks like a badass deep into her sixties, all six feet of her. She's a bit heavier, her already generous curves accentuated, and lines have invaded her face, but she still has that spikey inch-long bleach-blond hair and is still wearing form-fitting jeans and a black sweater. Her full lips quirk into a smile when she sees me as she stands up with pruners in her hand.

It's a cool afternoon in Seattle and the older woman is tending to some rose bushes in front of a verdant yard full of maple and ficus trees. The house beyond is small and looks to be old but is very well cared for, the wooden siding in good shape and the tan paint looking fresh.

Jessica wasn't hard to find. Took just a few minutes of searching. I emailed my employer, telling them I needed a few days to recover and find another place to live. I had a cheerful breakfast with my parents, the egg quite cold and God knows there would be no using the microwave to heat them up seeing how I came down late for breakfast.

I hardly noticed. I told them I had to go to Seattle, that I still had a few things in storage that would help with my recovery from losing everything.

I Ubered to the airport, buying a ticket for way too much money on the way. I hardly noticed that.

In my mind it was all Mia. The two years since her death and the year of hell with her cancer erased in my brain. The possibility of seeing her again whole and healthy and knowing me was all I could think of.

And, yes, it is something of a fevered dream I am having. The dream of seeing her one more time. Of holding her hand. Kissing her. Hugging her. Telling her how important she is to me.

I was never shy about telling Mia what she meant to me. I'm a gangly geek who collects toys, plays video games, and has a greying ponytail and a face that I can only describe charitably as plain. She's a goddess with exotic looks, long sleek limbs, hair as black as midnight, and beautifully dark skin.

I told her what she meant to me many times when she was sick and dying. I thought I knew how hard her loss would be, but how could I? Now that I know, I want one more chance to tell her what she meant, how she made my life worth living.

Part of me knows that after I see her again, I'll want just another "one more time," that it will never be enough, but my longing for her has blossomed again after traipsing through her young life.

And up to the moment I see Jessica again, I didn't know it had been real. But now that I see her... My life has purpose again. It has meaning. And that purpose and that meaning is Mia.

I open my mouth to speak, but Jessica strides up to me, takes my face in her hands, and kisses me hard. With tongue. And it's awfully familiar and a tad aggressive for my taste and my mouth is still sore from when she punched me in 1996, but... wow.

My mind on Mia, my body responding to Jessica, my aging hormones spinning out of control, I just gasp. I drop my backpack which contains my black duster and my cat fighting squirt guns.

"It's about time you got here," she says when we part. Her blue eyes are sparkling, and her smile shows more than a little bit of amusement.

I swallow and my nose is full of Jessica's flowery scent. I open my mouth to speak, to ask her the question I came to ask, but I can't talk.

She laughs; it's a bright, light sound that doesn't seem to go with the woman I met twenty-three years ago that would do anything to see her father one more time.

My hand goes to my mouth where she kissed me, the sensation lingering. It has been decades since any woman but Mia kissed me. I feel the burn of my healing scratches and I know it was all real. I sway there on the grass, pulling in huge breaths of moist air, smelling the grass and the flowers, being so glad to be out of the desert.

"Real," I mutter. "It was all real."

Jessica grabs my arm and it's clear that she's still quite strong. "Yeah, Ash, it's real. Sorry Angelica left you like that, but you know she always has her reasons."

Jessica has a quirky but compassionate smile playing on her full lips.

"Ash," I say, a goofy smile on my face as my mind tries to grasp what is going on. I love it that she called me Ash. I never asked that of Mia. Why didn't I do that?

"That's your name, isn't it?" she asks, her wrinkled forehead furrowing deeply.

"Yeah," I say, my goofy grin getting even bigger. "Ash is my name."

One eyebrow goes up as she studies me and my mind goes back to Angelica Huston and finding Mia again.

"Umm... I.... Have you...?" I stammer, trying to ask her if she ever saw Angelica Huston again, if the corgi came back a week later in 1996 for her.

Her smile is bright. "Yes. She's waiting for you." She nods towards a gate that leads to the backyard. I take a step towards it and she slaps me on the ass and laughs at my horrified look.

"It's good to see you again, Ash," she says.

I remember that I never told her my name, much less my nickname. I start to wonder how she can know and then I remember time travel and how we are all at different stages in our journey.

"Did we...?" I manage to say, wondering at the kiss and the familiar slap of my posterior.

She laughs and shakes her head. "Just go see her. She's had a bad day. Be gentle."

I walk slowly around to the backyard which is wide open grass with plenty of room. There is no spaceship visible, but Angelica Huston is lying in the middle of the yard, apparently asleep.

She looks so normal. Just a corgi, with radar ears, short legs, and a beautiful tan and white coat lying in the grass taking a nap, her nose twitching and her feet moving as if she is having a dream and running. She whimpers and I get down on the damp grass next to her and gently pet her.

She wakes with a start, sucking in a deep breath. She stands up, backs up a step, and it looks like she is about to bark at me, her lip pulling up into a snarl, but then she relaxes.

"Ashton Bach!" she says loudly in my mind. "I am glad you are here. I... I lost... I lost the ship to our enemies and only you can help me get it back."

I smile at first, the telepathic dog's upper crust English accent comfortingly familiar, but then my smile fades as I register what she said.

Only I can help? The middle-aged geek whose only innovative thought was to use squirt guns against alien felines. She needs me?

I came here to talk her into taking me back to see Mia, not to go on some crazy adventure after rampaging time-traveling cats.

And then it hits me. This is time travel, after all. There is quite literally time for me to help Angelica Huston *and* go see Mia again. There is time enough for adventure and time enough for love.

And maybe this version of Angelica Huston talked to an older version of me after this was all over and knows how I'm involved. It may twist your mind, but the adventures never stop.

"Tell me everything you know," I say, a smile back on my face.

CHAPTER SEVENTEEN

THE TALE ANGELICA HUSTON spins is, frankly, hard to follow. As I expect the tale I am telling you might be. Time travel is like that as cause and effect dances together in ways that do not appear to be linear, or even connected sometimes. But it is. There is cause and effect if you untangle the strands and view time subjectively instead of objectively.

In Angelica Huston's subjective timeline, it's been over a year since the two of us were together, although it's only been days for me. Not to mention the decades it has been for Jessica.

In that time, the corgi continued to run missions, rising past her first time-travel mission with me up the ranks of her kind until she was trusted with more and more important missions.

She traveled across the timeline and around the world in ways that I couldn't understand. Her missions weren't things like stopping world wars, but more along the lines of what she did with me, helping small things work out the way they should.

"Big changes," she says at one point, "are even beyond my people's ability to fully fathom. But small important things, it is there we can make a difference. If we but take care of the small things, the big things take care of themselves."

That cats were always there, always dogging her path, trying to steal her ship, trying to gain control of the most powerful technology in the universe.

Until the cats recruited someone with knowledge of Angelica, of the ship, who had witnessed the corgi flying it, who understood how it worked.

"It was you, Ashton Bach," the dog says in my head, her English accented voice quavering. "It was you that helped steal my ship. An older version of you. A future version of you from your perspective."

Her deep brown eyes stare at me as the shock of it washes over me and the moisture of the damp grass soaks through my jeans.

"And only you can help me get it back," she said. "And then, later, you must steal it from a past version of me so the timeline is not broken."

I FEEL like I've been thrust into a maelstrom of emotions. Wanting to see Mia again. Jessica's intimate greeting. Finding out that a future version of myself conspired with the felines to steal Angelica Huston's time-traveling spaceship. Knowing that I have to help her get it back again and then I have to steal it from her.

After our first adventure together, I thought I grokked this whole time-travel thing. I thought I had a clue about what was going on and wasn't a wet-behind-the-ears noob anymore.

Nope. Wrong. Not!

I am stumbling around Jessica's backyard, the corgi following on my heels. There are fruit trees here at the edge of the yard, cherry and peach, and a wooden fence that appears to be made out of redwood.

It's not a big yard, but it has a nice patio with worn metal furniture and a sliding glass door that shows a neat kitchen with granite counters and gleaming stainless-steel appliances.

My mind is grasping at the mundane to keep from being lost in that maelstrom of emotions. I am sweating in the cool damp weather, the T-shirt under my flannel sticking to my back.

"Why...?" I mumble. "Why would I do that?"

"That's what I need you to tell me," Angelica says in my head. When I turn around, she is sitting on the grass, her head cocked to one side, her radar ears pointed right at me.

"What did I say?" I ask. "How did it happen? How much older was I? Where was this? Why would I do that?"

"Calm down, big boy," Jessica says. She had come out into the yard and I hadn't noticed. She hands me a glass with a couple fingers of an amber-colored liquid. "Take a deep breath and drink this."

I like red wine, but don't drink that much. If there was an occasion to start drinking the hard stuff, though, this is it.

I take the glass and try to drink it all but end up coughing most of it up on the grass.

Jessica laughs and slaps me on the back as I'm bent there coughing. "You'll get better at it, Ash. Don't worry."

So we do know each other, in her past, my future? That means she knows something. She knows how this all turns out.

"Why did I do it?" I ask her when I can talk again, my chest tight and my breath coming fast.

Her blue eyes show compassion as she rubs her hand through her short bleach-blond hair, but she shakes her head. "Not how this works, babe. I'm sorry. And besides, you didn't tell me that much about it."

Now my mind is blazing back to when I asked Angelica how time travel worked. I mean, I am a lover of sci-fi, and if you are to succeed at the time-travel game, you've got to understand the rules.

Except Angelica didn't give me hard rules, saying my ape brain couldn't fathom it. I do know that we aren't living in a universe where every choice spawns another version of the multiverse, that many time-travel jumps into the past are just doing what has already been done.

I also know that big enough changes can fork the timeline and bring another version of reality into existence.

But which kind were we looking at? Angelica said I must steal the ship again (well... for the first time for me) so that indicates the former, but if the cats have the world's most powerful technology in their possession, what kind of havoc can they wreak?

"Deep breaths," Jessica says. I'm kneeling on the damp

grass and I don't remember how I got there, my breath coming in huge gasps, my chest feeling so very tight.

Angelica is licking my hand. "You're a good ape," she says gently in my head. "I know you can do this. Buck up now and let's crack on."

I'm having a panic attack. It's too much.

Jessica pulls me into a hug and her strong arms are a comfort and disturbingly familiar. "Shhhh," she whispers as she begins to rock me gently and starts humming the theme song from *The Never Ending Story*, one of my favorite movies as a kid.

She does know me. She really knows me. I relax into her arms and feel my chest loosening. And the magic of Angelica Huston's doggy saliva does its part too, just like the last time we were together.

"Don't think about it, Ash," Jessica says. "Just tell me why that future you would help steal the ship. Say the first thing that comes to mind."

"Mia," I whisper, and feel bad saying her name while being held by another woman. "I came here to talk Angelica Huston into taking me to see an older Mia, one that knows me, so I could say goodbye again."

Jessica sniffs and holds me tighter, and I have to wonder if she ever got to see her father again.

CHAPTER EIGHTEEN

THERE'S someone else in Jessica's house. Someone watching us. I noticed it first when I was having my dramatic little panic attack out in Jessica's yard, a curtain moving in what looks to be a bedroom just enough so someone could peek out.

There seems to be an unspoken rule about telling those that are behind you in the time-traveling journey too much.

I'm sure that Jessica knows more than she is telling me, and I suspect that whoever is staying hidden knows plenty. But that's not how this works. I am doing this blind, without help from my future—which Jessica has experienced. And I guess the unspoken reason is so that the future turns out the same way it did the last time.

But why would they want me to help the cats steal Angelica Huston's spaceship again? Shouldn't that be something we actually change? And if we did, would that lead to an alternate reality and then in this reality the cats would still have the spaceship?

The infinitely recursive nature of it can just warp your mind. And when I meet the younger Jessica again—which it seems I must—I must not tell her too much about what I know of her future. Not that I know much at this point.

I think that's what makes this so hard to think about, much less write about. Our individual, subjective futures and pasts are all scrambled up and aren't in sync with the objective world.

"You with us, Ash?" Jessica asks. We are sitting at the table on her patio. It's made of black metal and has a pot of begonias on it. Apparently, Jessica likes to raise flowers when she's not skipping across the timeline and being a badass.

There's more whiskey in front of me and I've been taking the smallest sips possible. I can't say that I like how it tastes, but the burning warmth is nice and my brain is relaxing, just a bit.

I nod. Angelica Huston is just off the patio, sitting in the grass staring at me. In our first time-traveling adventure she kept thrusting me into situations with Mia without orientation or instructions. Now she is asking me how to get back a time-traveling spaceship from my future-self.

"So you wouldn't want to go back in time and see George Lucas filming *Star Wars* or anything like that?" she asks with a quirky little smile. "It would only be your wife Mia?"

I nod and really appreciate that she didn't use the past tense when referring to Mia or say "deceased" or anything like that.

"Come on, Ash," she says. "Use your words. Talk to us."

She isn't old enough to be my mother and I certainly don't like that maternal phrasing. I feel my cheeks flush, but say,

"Mia is the only thing, the only reason I can imagine doing something like that."

The chair under me is hard and uncomfortable and I am wishing that I had never come, that I was still wondering if it had all been a fevered dream.

I wish it had been.

"Look at me, babe," Jessica says and I do, her blue eyes drawing me in. She smiles and nods. "When would you have wanted to go? Where would you have wanted to go? This is important."

I lick my lips and nod back to her. "I... towards the end I..." I can't hold her gaze and take another small sip of whiskey, finding it easier to drink now. I look down at my hands and continue. "I lost it a few days before she died. She was in hospice. In our home. She was bedridden and not with it very much. I..."

I surge up, the memory too strong, too bitter, the metal chair scraping on the cement. I wander out into the yard, both of them following.

"You can do this, Ash," Angelica says in my head. "I know you can."

I nod but don't look at either of them, my arms wrapped around my chest as if I'm trying to give myself a hug.

"We had battled her cancer for over a year," I continue, "and it was clear we were going to lose. Pancreatic cancer ain't no walk in the park. She was asleep more and more, her breath rattling as her lungs filled with fluid. It was the rattling. I couldn't take it anymore. Mia's parents were there, her brother was there. I just walked out and got in my car and drove. I didn't even know where I was going. I ended up near Portland before I got myself under control."

I look at them and they both have such compassion in their eyes. Jessica's blues and Angelica Huston's browns. I feel tears stinging my cheeks and I wipe them away and turn, pacing over the soft grass some more.

"She rallied while I was gone," I say. "Her last rally. She was briefly awake and lucid. She said her goodbyes to her family. And I missed it. She was in a coma when I finally got back and she never woke up again."

I feel the tightening of my chest and the quickening of my breath, but I hold the panic attack at bay this time. I never spoke about this before. To anyone. Mia's family knows, but we never talked about it and I hadn't seen them since I moved away from Seattle. I hadn't told my parents or anyone else, but I just told Jessica Cole and a telepathic alien dog.

This is my shame and I would give almost anything to go back and be with her during her rally. To look in her beautiful brown eyes once more and tell her how much I love her, how much she means to me. Tell her that I'll be okay, that she can give up the terrible fight and be at peace.

And, apparently, I *will* do almost anything, including help steal Angelica Huston's time-traveling spaceship, to go back to that day.

I take a deep breath and all the thoughts swirling through my mind come together and form a picture. A strange picture, but not one I can say no to. If I can help Angelica Huston find her spaceship, take it back from the cats, then at some point in my future I'll have the opportunity to steal it and go see Mia.

It doesn't feel right, twisted like it is, but it is what I need and it is what Angelica Huston needs.

I straighten up and feel my nerves steadying. For Mia I can do this. To right that wrong, I can do this. To be free of that shame, I can do this.

I feel a brief stab of guilt. I am going to do another wrong—steal her ship—to right my wrong with Mia. But then again, I am going to right that wrong before I do it. Subjectively, in my timeline, of course. This time-travel thing totally puts the notion of karma on its ear.

I turn and they are both staring at me, their eyes widening as they see the determination on my face. "It was August 23, 2017," I say. "At our house in Clyde Hill. I left just before midnight. That is when and that is where we need to go. The ship will be there."

They are both still just staring at me.

"I brought my duster and squirt guns," I say, feeling my energy shift towards something manic. "They're in my backpack. Let me get dressed." I turn towards Jessica. "Do you have any cayenne, or something hotter? Water is not enough against those cats anymore."

They are both still staring at me.

And then it hits me. The cats stole the spaceship. "Wait. How do we get there?"

"Well that," Angelica says in my head, "is going to be something of a trick."

CHAPTER NINETEEN

THE ALIENS from the star Sirius, the intelligent telepathic canines, are spread out across the galaxy doing their work on many planets with intelligent life. It's not clear to me if domesticated dogs are the exact same species as these, but the link is unmistakable. I mean, your dogs don't speak to you telepathically, do they?

I am, admittedly, a dog person. Mia and I always had dogs. Our last dog, Misty, died days after Mia did. She was old, but not *that* old. I think the poor girl died of a broken heart. I haven't been able to even think about getting another one. That and moving back to Phoenix and living in an apartment. A dog, especially the bigger ones, need room to run. And a door... a dog needs a dog door so they can take care of their basic elimination needs unencumbered.

But I'm rambling again, aren't I?

Okay. So, the canines are spread out and they have limited technology for their mission on Earth.

There are a number of ships involved in their study of human biology. Angelica Huston was chief human abductor for English-speaking countries before she moved to the time-travel mission.

You know, it kind of makes sense. Since the canines have been the ones abducting and studying humans, it explains all the anal probing stories what with dog's fascination with sniffing butts.

But the time-travel mission is new and there is only one of those spaceships on Earth. Angelica's. The one I helped the cats steal.

Jessica and I are back at the patio table and Angelica is sitting in the grass again, having just explained this to me. I take another warming sip of the whiskey, the sharp scent starting to become more enticing.

"So how do we get there?" I ask.

Angelica pants like she is a normal dog and Jessica shrugs. They are the pros here, surely they have an idea.

But they don't.

"You've studied the fictional literature you apes have constructed on time travel, Ash," Angelica says in my mind. "And I must say, as a species, you are quite enamored with it. What do you suggest?"

Fiction is the answer to our quandary? But how?

In *Back to the Future Part II*, Marty McFly weaves in and out of the same events his past-self had just experienced. And it sounds like that was part of the idea here, I had to take back the ship from my future-self.

In *Edge of Tomorrow* and *Groundhog Day*, the timeline

resets every time the protagonist dies so they can improve themselves, but that doesn't seem to help.

In H. G. Wells's *The Time Machine*, which popularized the concept of time travel, our protagonist goes forward in time and his ship is stolen, but the Morlocks don't use the time machine and getting it back isn't all that complicated.

I run through more examples in my head. *Harry Potter and the Prisoner of Azkaban*. Stephen King's *11/22/63*. Mark Twain's *A Connecticut Yankee in King Arthur's Court*. And a bunch more.

Jessica is watching me, an amused smile on her face.

"What?" I ask.

She shrugs and it's a sensual gesture for her, even at her age. "I like to watch you think."

"This isn't fair," I say.

"What isn't fair?" she asks with a smile that is the opposite of innocent.

"You. Flirting," I say. "You clearly know things."

"Am I flirting with you, Ash?" she asks, a smile playing on her full lips.

Time travel was the reason that Mia and I got together. I know that after my time with Angelica Huston. It was my presence in her young life as a middle-aged man that made her subconsciously recognize me as a young man. That and me giving my younger self the nudge he needed to go talk to her.

Now it was looking like there was something between Jessica and me (the "was" being from Jessica's perspective, not mine) and there would be something between us from my perspective. Was this another relationship that existed (will exist?) only because of time travel and the strange weaving together of our subjective experiences?

Right now, she knows more about our relationship than I do, but at some point, I will know more. I can't fathom what has passed between us, or how I ever got enough distance from Mia to move on, but my future-self will completely understand it.

I'm getting a little lost in Jessica's blue eyes and feeling guilty about it when I realize I've gone on yet another long tangent in my strange brain about time-traveling romances. I look away and shake my head to snap myself out of it.

I don't know the solution to this problem, but my future-self will. I can't help, but my future-self can. Or Angelica's future-self. Or Jessica's past-self, because I'm pretty sure she knows the answer but is just letting us figure it out so this doesn't turn into some Möbius strip of logic with no beginning and no end.

I stand and clear my throat, a brief wave of dizziness rippling through me. I've had more of that whiskey than I thought. "This is time travel," I begin. "Our future-selves will take us to where we need to go." I gesture to the yard, and now that I am looking at it, I can see that it has a large open area perfect for Angelica's spaceship to land, the only trees around the edges of the yard.

"We will be here at any moment," I say.

I make a grand flourish, I blame the whiskey for that, but nothing happens. No spaceship appears. The seconds tick by and I can hear the sound of a car passing out on the street and Angelica Huston panting. I see the curtain to the bedroom open a crack again as our mysterious watcher observes.

But nothing happens. No spaceship. No future-selves coming to rescue us, just my heart pounding loudly in my ears.

I collapse back into the metal chair and sigh.

"So dramatic, Ash," Jessica says with a broad smile. "So, I guess our future-selves are lame. What's next?"

CHAPTER TWENTY

"WELL THAT IS THAT...," Angelica begins, her bright British accent sounding deflated and defeated in my mind as she sits on the grass, her soulful brown eyes staring at me. "I can contact the abduction pack and they can send word to Sirius. My time-travel career will be over, but we will get help and it will be on time."

Of course. Another time-traveling ship could swoop in and stop the cats (and me) from stealing her ship in the first place.

But if they do that, surely that will change the timeline and I won't steal the ship and I won't get to see Mia. Or they'll get the ship back right after she loses it and I won't get to see Mia.

The corgi gets up and shakes and trots away.

"No!" I yell before I've thought it through. Angelica stops and turns, looking at me. I'm on my feet, clearly ready to rush after her even though I don't know what I'm saying yet. "Wait. There's a way. I know there is a way for us to get it back."

"What is it then?" Jessica asks from behind me.

Her voice is hushed, almost reverent. Is this it, then? The moment she heard about. That a future me told her about? Where I utter something brilliant, all those hours spent immersed in sci-fi and fantasy paying off?

Except now I'm thinking about being brilliant and can't think of a thing.

"Ash?" Angelica asks in my head.

I'm pacing on the lush grass, both of them watching me, mumbling my thoughts to get Jessica's expectant tone out of my head. I suddenly understand why you don't want to hint at the future to those that haven't seen it yet. Being told is an entirely different experience than figuring it out yourself.

"Our future-selves didn't come rescue us," I say as my feet pad over the soft grass. "That just means we found another way. But what way? You can't catch up with a time-traveling spaceship without a time-traveling spaceship. And there is only one time-traveling spaceship on Earth."

I stop in my tracks, smile, and turn around. "There is only one time-traveling spaceship on Earth," I say.

Angelica cocks her head. "Yes, Ash. And you stole it."

I nod, feeling my cheeks flush. "But let's assume we get it back. I mean, we have to, don't we? The world hasn't radically changed into some kind of cat's paradise, has it?"

Jessica snorts. "Have you looked at the stats on money spent on pets? And besides, how would you know if the world has changed?"

"But Angelica Huston would," I say, turning to the corgi. "You would, wouldn't you?"

She pants for a moment and I don't think she heard me, but then I notice her unfocused eyes and realize that she is just thinking.

"Given that we all still remember my ship," she says, "and that we are all still here, I would have to assume that we retrieved the ship."

I file that away to reconcile later with the hints of how time travel works and nod. "Right. And that means you have possession of the spaceship in your future."

Angelica pants at me. Maybe that is the same as a human nod.

"And since our future-selves aren't coming to us," I say, "we need to go to them."

Jessica is conspicuously quiet behind me, which makes me suspect that I am on the right track.

"And how does that help us, Ash?" the dog asks.

I shove my hands into my jean pockets and stare at the grass. I'm faking this. Pulling at one promising idea at a time. There is a way. I know it, but how to find it?

And then it all clicks into focus.

"Did you have any upcoming missions that will bring you to this time?"

Angelica is quiet, panting again. If she didn't, we are screwed. If she does then this just might work out. Do intelligent alien canines have good memories? Would she retain details of a mission she had only heard briefly about? Did she get missions in groups or just one at a time? And, actually, besides helping old geeks like me, what were her missions like?

"I am sorry, Ash," she says in my head. "I only get one mission briefing at a time. Things can change, you know. The nature of time travel."

I feel my body sagging. I am out of ideas and that means no Mia, no righting that wrong, no saying goodbye properly to the love of my life.

A slight breeze kicks up and the smell of flowers fills my nose. I have my back to the corgi and Jessica, staring at the grass.

"But, you know, there was this past mission," Angelica begins. "It was quite odd because my ship was not exactly where I left it."

I turn and I see that Jessica is smiling and Angelica has her head cocked and is staring at me.

"No one can get in that ship besides me," Angelica continues. "So how could it move?"

I step right into the opening. "Because a future version of you moved it."

She barks and it's a loud and joyful thing. "It was a brief domestic mission in a small town in Colorado in..." she trails off and pants again. My heart starts beating hard and I'm just sure this is going to work. "...in four of your ape hours," she finishes.

CHAPTER TWENTY-ONE

WHILE I'M TRYING to figure out how the hell you get from Seattle, Washington, to Colorado in four hours, Angelica Huston trots off around the house without a word and is soon out of sight.

"Where's she going?" I ask, taking a step across the yard to follow her.

"Don't bother," Jessica says from the patio.

"What?" I ask.

"Don't bother," she repeats. "The old girl always keeps a few tricks to herself."

"But we've got to get to Colorado," I say.

Jessica smiles and nods. "Yes you do."

I take another step towards where Angelica went and what Jessica said sinks in. I stop and turn. "You're not coming?"

She smiles, the lines gathering around her eyes making me quite sure that this Jessica Cole smiles a whole lot more than the one I met twenty-three years ago. "No..." she says, rather vaguely.

I'm not a first-time time traveler anymore, so it clicks in my mind. "But a younger version of you is?"

She shrugs noncommittally. "I'm retired." She takes a sip of her whiskey and gestures around her well-manicured yard. "And be gentle with my younger self when you meet her. She hasn't had good friends for as long as I have."

I just stare at her. There is so much more she could tell me, but that is all she will. And now I'm quite sure that the older Jessica Cole knows exactly how this all turns out.

"Where did Angelica go?" I ask, my mind back to Colorado which leads to getting Angelica's ship back, which leads to me seeing Mia.

"She's summoning the pack," she says, getting up with a sigh. "The crew she used to command. The ship is too big to pick you guys up here. Let's get you some hot sauce and get moving."

I follow her through the sliding glass door into the kitchen. The room is very neat, but clearly well used with an array of appliances all a bright cheery red and lots of glass jars lining the granite countertops containing a colorful variety of beans and grains.

The floors are tiled and the appliances are stainless steel. Blooming potted flowers crowd the little kitchen table for space.

My backpack is there and she nods towards a bottle of habanero hot sauce sitting on the counter. "I believe that will do."

She leans against the counter, her arms folded as she

watches me pull out all my squirt guns and fill them up. The last time we met, she was on the side of the cats and had a real gun and I was using these on her.

The kitchen has an open floor plan and the tile ends with the carpet of a sparsely furnished living area. On the tile I see a blue ceramic dog bowl with water in it and wonder about it. Who is hiding here? And if she has a dog, why keep it hidden? But Jessica isn't really telling me much, but there is one thing she might talk about.

"Did you get to see your dad again?" I ask quietly. It was what she wanted twenty-three years ago, what the cats dangled to get her help.

She sighs behind me, but I don't turn to look. "I did," she says, her voice hushed.

I know she can't—or won't—tell me much, but as I'm at the sink filling up my water guns looking out onto her lovely backyard, I ask, "Any advice for me?"

"I know you don't believe this now," she says, her voice soft. "But sometimes the past is best left in the past."

INTERLAKEN PARK IS dense forest and verdant green and not that far of a walk from Jessica's home. The sun has just set and I breathe deeply of the scent, the moist earthy smell of the forest. Something you never smell in Phoenix.

I've got my black duster on, and my array of habanero-dosed squirt guns stowed and at the ready. I don't feel like Ashton Bach, the widowed middle-aged geek. I feel like Ash, the time-traveling cat warrior. Well... my weapons are just squirt guns, sure, but I did defend the world's most powerful technology against a determined pack of cats with them.

Our walk is mostly silent and I suspect she fears giving more away. She's not told me much, just hinted—rather enthusiastically—that we will be / have been / are in some kind of relationship.

Sorry, but verbs are just impossible. For her it seems the correct verb is we "have been" in a relationship. For me, the correct verb seems to be "will be." And by her easy intimacy with me, that makes me suspect that "are" could also apply.

All of these tenses apply at once because of time travel. It changes everything.

Jessica is an attractive woman, both in her forties when I first met her and in her sixties like she is now. She is also clearly intelligent and loves to cultivate beauty, but she's not Mia. I will admit that my body responded to her, both times we've met, but that's just stupid hormones. But then again it was stupid hormones and probably pheromones that attracted me to Mia the first time I saw her.

"Can you tell me if this all works out?" I ask, my curiosity finally making me talk. We're off the narrow road that circles the park and onto a thin trail that looks more like an animal trail, the close trees causing us to duck as we walk.

"You and me," she asks from in front of me, some amusement in her voice, "or saying goodbye to Mia?"

I swallow hard and think that maybe she's flirting like this to keep me off balance, to keep me from guessing what's coming. I clear my throat and say, "Mia." It comes out as a croak.

She turns and her cheeks are flushed, so there goes my

theory of this just being about keeping me off balance. "Let me give you some advice, Ashton," she says, spitting out my full name for the first time. "Don't miss what's right in front of you because of the past you think was so damn perfect."

She's staring at me, her fists on her hips, her lips pursed. I open my mouth to speak, but what the hell am I supposed to say? She has a past with me that I don't have with her. But I'm starting to get angry about it, so I say, "Are you what's right in front of me, Jessica?"

"I guess I am." She blinks and her shoulders fall and then she turns. "And you are what is behind me." She strides off into the forest and I rush after her.

WE DON'T TALK ANYMORE. I have to work to keep up with Jessica's long strides until we end up in a small clearing. I'm confused, because it's smaller than Jessica's backyard. Angelica Huston is sitting in the clearing staring up into the quickly darkening sky.

"What are we doing here?" I ask.

The corgi looks at me. "Hitching a ride, of course. Put your thumb out like a good ape. Isn't that the universal gesture required for this circumstance?"

I turn to ask Jessica if she knows anything, but I just catch a glimpse of her disappearing into the forest the way we came. It seems there is unfinished business there, but I shake it off. It doesn't feel like *my* unfinished business. At least not yet.

"Thumb out, Ash," Angelica says, and I swear she's smiling at me, but that could just be the dimming light. Is this some kind of canine protocol? Am I signaling my willingness to other alien canines to be part of this adventure?

I take a deep breath and smile. Glad to be clear of Jessica and whatever all of that was. I feel like Arthur Dent in *The Hitchhiker's Guide to the Galaxy* as I stick my thumb out.

The corgi barks and I feel like an invisible hand just closed around me and I'm suddenly floating, my feet leaving the ground, the corgi floating next to me.

She barks again and I smile wide until the nausea hits me and then I close my eyes and clamp my mouth shut. I may look like Neo—granted, a middle-aged one with a greying ponytail—but I'm not acting like him anymore, just trying to keep my food down and survive whatever the hell this is.

I slit my eyes open and see trees below my feet and then the streets of Seattle as we rise up into the air. Time travel was something I was expecting, not this whole Peter Pan routine. But no, I'm not flying, I'm being held, lifted, raised. This is more like a tractor beam. I'm in a sci-fi adventure here, after all, not a fantasy adventure.

And yes, this is how I deal with my fear and my disorientation, by evaluating the experience and comparing it to my core, albeit geeky, literature. So, thinking Star Trek, not Peter Pan, I look up and see... Well, I don't see much of anything. There is a dense layer of darkening clouds above us, this is Seattle, after all, and nothing else.

But there has to be something, so as I stare, I notice that the portion of clouds right above us doesn't look quite right. Well, they look like clouds, but the pattern isn't the same as the rest of the clouds. And that slightly off pattern has a shape, like a thick stick with bulbous ends... no, like a dog bone.

I smile and am suddenly over my nausea. I am in some kind of force field being drawn up to the canine mother ship. Because it's clear that this spaceship is much larger than Angelica Huston's.

This must be the pack that Angelica summoned. Her former crew that is abducting and studying humans.

I make the mistake of looking down. We are hundreds of feet in the air, the city growing smaller right below my feet. I shut my eyes and swallow against the returning nausea and let the four-footed aliens take me.

CHAPTER TWENTY-TWO

I PASS out at some point as I'm floating above Seattle towards the canine spaceship. I mean I must have, because I wake up in a small room with puppies licking me. A whole bunch of puppies all around with wagging tails and enthusiastic tongues. Brown ones, white ones, tan ones. Some no bigger than my hand and others as big as ten pounds.

I laugh and pet them as they wriggle all over me. My laughter is full and genuine and I actually sound happy.

And then I remember where I am and what I am supposed to be doing. I'm aboard a spaceship from the star Sirius and my mission is to help Angelica Huston, a telepathic corgi, rescue her time-traveling spaceship that I will steal in my subjective future.

Right. I go back to laughing and playing with puppies, their clean puppy smell filling my nose, their sweet kisses making me happy.

I do notice that I'm in a small grey room with no sharp

edges and the floor beneath me is soft, just like in Angelica's ship.

It once again occurs to me that these alien canines have spiked saliva because I really am just so happy. I'm not worried about Mia or Jessica. About missions or cats using time travel to remake the world in their image, or anything of the sort.

And, if I'm being honest, these are some of the happiest moments of my life. It is just the simple pleasure of puppies with not another thought in my head.

But soon a round opening appears in the room and Angelica Huston is there. She barks once and the puppies leave me and I immediately miss the touch of their soft, warm fur.

"Hello, Angelica Huston," I say, a silly grin on my face.

"Hello, Ashton Bach," Angelica says in my head. "It's time for your examination, if you would please follow me."

This might be a bigger ship, but the passageways are dog sized so I am soon crawling behind the corgi, glad for the padded surfaces. "Examination?" I ask.

"Yes," she says. "That is the mission of this vessel, to further understand the biological properties of homo sapiens. It is a wonder of the universe that you violent apes have been so successful here."

"So, like a checkup?" I ask cheerfully, clearly still under the influence of the puppy saliva.

"Yes," she says. "A very thorough checkup. Think of it as the price of your passage."

I could care less and am just fascinated by every little thing. The small grates on the curved walls that Angelica sniffs as we go by. The other dogs that trot past us, a lanky dalmatian, a tan dingo-looking dog, and a white-and-black pit bull. Angelica has a brief barking conversation with the pit bull that ends in the smaller corgi emitting a low, dangerous growl as the pit bull sniffs me.

The larger dog slinks off with its tail between its legs and I recall that Angelica used to command this ship.

We end up in a small room just large enough for a human-sized examination table and one of those low platforms with four paw-sized holes like I saw Angelica controlling her spaceship with.

And then I notice that dangling apparatus hanging from the ceiling. Twisting tubes, some with sharp needles, others with bulbous ends. Angelica mounts the platform and the tubes spring to life like some kind of strange sea anemone.

Visions of bizarre stories of alien abduction and anal probing fill my mind. Angelica told me about this before, but I don't think it fully sank in. All the stories have the gray aliens with big eyes, but maybe it's the soulful dog eyes people see under the influence of some heavy-duty doggy saliva that created those impressions.

"Yeah," I say, the twisting instruments sobering me up a bit. "You know. I think we can skip the exam."

Angelica looks at me, her brown eyes penetrating, like they're looking into my soul. "I will be gentle, Ash," she says. "You can rest assured of that. We will be in your state of Colorado by the time we are done."

"Can't we just... you know... say you did it?" I ask. Believe me, that puppy saliva is still doing its job or I would have just been freaking out.

"Please, Ash," she says gently. "Remove your garments and lie down on the table. It won't hurt, you can count on this."

"Promise?" I ask.

"Yes," she says. "You are my friend, Ash." And I can hear it in her voice, there is a rift between us that my future-self created when he stole her ship. That this is something of a test. Even though my stealing of her ship is in my future, it is in her past.

I nod and smile, letting the puppy saliva do its thing as I take off my duster. For Mia, I will do this. So I can see Mia again.

CHAPTER TWENTY-THREE

INTERSPECIES RELATIONSHIPS ARE HARD. I've always thought that when it came to the dogs I have had in my life. They are wired differently. They look at the world differently. They react differently.

Taking the descendant of a wild wolf and asking it to be a happy, healthy, docile member of your home is a big ask. It asks a lot of the dog and a lot of the ape.

Sorry. Angelica's constant referring to us as apes has really sunk in. It's humbling in a way to think of us as evolved apes. And as I look at how mad this world is, it seems we could use that kind of humbling.

So, yeah, interspecies relationships are hard. And I thought this before I knew dogs were aliens and some of them very intelligent and telepathic.

How does this relate to my "examination" you might ask?

Well, dogs quite clearly have different boundaries when it comes to physicality. And yes, I am speaking of how they are always sniffing each other's butts but also how they lick (themselves and others) and have a pack mentality. They don't have the same kind of sense of personal space us apes have.

I'm not going to detail my time on the table, all the probing and sampling and high-tech dog-style sniffing. I will say it was thorough and Angelica was true to her word and it was gentle and it didn't hurt, but it certainly wasn't comfortable. Physically or psychologically.

And it didn't feel appropriate, but from the intelligent telepathic canine's perspective I'm sure it was.

See what I said about interspecies relationships? All this time we humans have been looking to the stars to find intelligent alien life and it's been here among us all along.

"What is the difference between you and the dogs that have been my…" I say, having trouble finding the right words.

Angelica Huston and I are in another small room. It looks like all the others with soft grey walls and rounded corners. I can smell the strange, barely there scents I remember from being on Angelica's other ship—the canines communicating complex information through smell. With the dreaded examination table out of sight and these thoughts rolling around my head, I find myself having to talk.

"Pets?" Angelica asks.

I shake my head. "I have never liked that word. I was looking for another one. Like 'companion' maybe."

The corgi seems to sigh and I hear her say in my head, "This will be hard for your ape brain to absorb, but if this is important to you, I will try to explain."

I nod. "Please."

Angelica pauses and licks my hand briefly and I feel my

mind sharpen, the dullness from all the puppy licking fading away.

It occurs to me that I am asking a lot of her, that she likely views this conversation as a way more intimate act than what happened in the examination room.

"Your canine companions," she begins, her voice in my head taking on a thoughtful tone and the words coming slowly. "They are the same species as I am. But... well, this is the hard part."

"What?" I ask.

"The first of us that came to this planet centuries ago, they were the best of us, Ash," she says. "They accepted a greatly shortened life and blocked off the most powerful parts of their minds so they could be of service to you apes. They changed themselves and their offspring to maximize their ability to be of service to your kind."

I nod slowly. I am a dog person, so this is one of the easiest things to believe that my time with Angelica has presented me with. People like me, we are way better off with a dog in our lives. With a loving being that forces us out of our own heads and our own selfish nature because they need us.

But knowing that they chose this, that they gave up so much just to be with us...?

Tears roll down my cheeks and I feel no shame, whatsoever. I got my first dog a couple of years before I met Mia. A copper-colored cocker spaniel named Winston.

Sure, it took me time traveling back to the bar I met Mia in to give my shy younger self the nudge he needed to go talk to Mia, but it was Winston that transformed me into a decent human being with his affection and playful nature and his absolute need of me.

Without Winston, I would not have been good enough for Mia—although I still doubt that I was good enough, but you get the point.

"This is what I wish for myself," Angelica says in my head. "I wish to be worthy of being an ape's companion."

"Even though you won't be able to talk and time travel and everything?" I ask. I'm a sci-fi geek, so to me there is nothing cooler than what Angelica already is.

"Yes, Ashton Bach," she says in my head. "This is why it's so important that we get the ship back. Being an ape's companion is the highest honor one of my kind can achieve on this planet."

"Well," I begin with a grin. "You are my companion, Angelica Huston. The best companion that I could hope for."

And then Angelica is in my lap, licking my neck, her tail wagging vigorously and I pet her warm body and for a few moments there everything is good.

CHAPTER TWENTY-FOUR

ANGELICA HUSTON and I are dropped off in a thick forest full of towering ponderosa pine trees and a few stubby scrub oaks. The air is cool and fresh and I can smell the faint scent of vanilla from the pines.

Don't ask me, I have no idea why pine trees smell like vanilla. I've heard some people say they smell like strawberries, but I don't get that at all. Maybe pine trees are like a Rorschach test for your nose. For me it's vanilla and I love it.

The forest reminds me of Flagstaff, Arizona, with the preponderance of pines, but the oaks are more bush-like and I don't see the characteristic volcanic rocks that are all around Flagstaff.

We are somewhere near Pagosa Springs, Colorado, where a past Angelica Huston is about to park her time-traveling spaceship to go on what she called a domestic mission.

Maybe she's pretending to be a stray to open an ape's heart.

I mean, my heart is open. I will admit that my notion of how dogs and humans relate was, admittedly, a rather romantic one. But now that I know the truth, now that I know what the dogs gave up and all the abuse many of them are subject to amongst us, I want to rescue dogs all day long. I want to make sure every single one is cared for and loved.

Yeah, let's face it, once this time-travel madness is over, I'm going to get a small house with a huge yard and become an eccentric dog man.

But for now, it's me and Angelica, creeping through the forest on our way to steal past-Angelica's spaceship.

"Down! Quiet!" Angelica yells in my head. It's not fair, she's telepathic, so no one can hear her shouting at me.

I crouch behind a pine tree breathing in the sweet scent and watch as a reflective bone-shaped craft gently hovers to a landing in a small clearing of trees.

I've never seen the craft moving from the outside. It's utterly silent and eerily graceful, making our human technology seem utterly childlike.

A round opening appears on the smooth surface of the ship and a corgi hops out and trots away, the opening closing behind her.

Now, I'm not a person that would say that one corgi looks just like the next. Their markings are unique, like a fingerprint, but this corgi looks exactly the same as Angelica Huston.

I know, I know. This was the plan, but seeing two versions of the same being at the same time is a little freaky. It's also pretty awesome. I mean, I've already interacted with a past version of myself, but it wasn't quite like this.

I feel like I've earned some kind of time-travel achievement badge: Stalk past version of being with current version of being.

We sit there for a few minutes until the past-Angelica is well out of sight. I figure it's the corgi radar ears, we don't want her to hear us stealing her ship.

Okay, so now ownership is getting tricky with this time-travel thing. This is, clearly, past-Angelica's ship, but does the Angelica I am with have any claim to it? Are we actually stealing past-Angelica's spaceship or is it a valid use by the current Angelica?

(Note: For sanity's sake, all past- future- current- references are from my perspective. Change your point of view in this story and all of that changes, bringing into question how well our language's tenses work when time travel is involved. I must ask Angelica at some point if the canine language has a better way of representing these things.)

And then Angelica is trotting off and the ship opens for her and we steal (or don't steal) past-Angelica's time-traveling spaceship which used to be current Angelica's time-traveling spaceship and will be stolen again by a future version of me, but for now we are going to use this stolen spaceship to get back her future stolen spaceship.

Yup. I'm a little dizzy thinking about it as we take off.

THE BRIDGE of Angelica's time-traveling spaceship is cramped for me. I sit leaning against the soft surface of the grey wall while Angelica is on the low platform with her four paws inserted into holes, a stalk right in front of her twitching nose as the ship communicates data to her through her superior olfactory senses.

The front of the bridge is a grainy black-and-white view looking down. A vast forest, a mountain range to the north, a small community built around lakes, roads, and a small twisting river running right through town. Makes me wish we had some time to explore Pagosa Springs.

But the view is brief as the Earth falls beneath us. I could be fooling myself, but we seem to be rising into orbit faster than the last time I did this with Angelica.

I know what's coming, but there is no way for me to brace myself. The black-and-white display shows the curve of the Earth and everything is still and so beautiful, but for just a moment. And then the Earth seems to shudder, going out of focus. My skin prickles like I just rolled in a patch of poison ivy, my stomach flips, and I smell burning plastic and I want nothing more than to throw up. The Earth shudders again, comes back in focus, and I let out a gasping sigh as my stomach finds its proper place in my abdomen.

I am so relieved that it's over, but then the cycle happens again. The Earth shudders, goes out of focus, and I feel sicker and smell burning plastic again. But it doesn't last long. The Earth shudders and comes back into focus.

I don't think much of it. Maybe this was a special kind of jump. Soon we are falling towards Earth, towards Seattle and our mission. It occurs to me that we haven't strategized or made a plan.

"How are we going to do this?" I ask. "Will I have to face

my future-self? How many cats do you think we'll be taking on? What happens if we fail?"

The questions come tumbling out. I have more, so many more, namely if I'll get a chance to go see Mia while we're here, but I clamp my mouth shut. I sound like an utter noob. And, I guess, I am. I mean, I've done some time traveling but it was little things, not like this.

"Hold on, Ashton Bach," Angelica says in my head, stress coming through her buttoned-up English accent. "Something isn't right."

I can see Puget Sound. I can see the dotting of islands and peninsulas and inlets. It's the same as when I first saw this view with Angelica. But wait. No. Something isn't right.

I see water and forest and...

That is all I see. There is no Seattle.

CHAPTER TWENTY-FIVE

OKAY, if I were to imagine the world remade around cats—and do keep in mind that I am a dog person—I would think that the world would be largely the same, but the human population would be more focused on cats. God would be a cat and everyone would pray to this cat god. Like the Egyptians with Bast, but in a monotheistic way. Humans would actively worship the cats in their homes and their homes would be even more cat-centric. And there'd be no dogs or any other kind of "pet," of course.

That is what I would imagine.

Not an empty world.

We land in Interlaken Park, the same place Angelica's pack picked us up. And it looks the same, a small grassy clearing amongst a thick, sweetly scented forest.

Angelica stands there right outside of the ship sniffing the air.

"Are we in the wrong time?" I ask.

"No, Ashton Bach," she says in my head, her tone rather stressed.

"Is this because of the double jump?" I ask, my tone very stressed.

"Double jump?" Angelica asks, her brown eyes looking up at me.

I nod. "Yeah, you know, when on your display, the Earth shudders, goes out of focus, and then I feel like I'm on a roller coaster, my skin is hot and itchy, and I smell burning plastic, and then the Earth comes back into focus. That happened twice."

She's staring at me, her nose twitching, as if there is something wrong with me and she's trying to smell it.

"Is that what you experienced?" she asks.

I nod. "Yeah. Every time, except it usually only happens once. It's the smell that's the worse, it lingers in the nose."

She tilts her head and looks up and to the left, her tail giving one restless swish.

"I think you should sit down, Ash," she says. Now her voice is gentle and stressed.

"But... shouldn't we get back to our mission?" I say. "We've got to get your ship back."

"We have all the time we need. Be a good ape and sit," she says in my head.

I sit down on the ground and the mulchy smell of it chases out the lingering scent of burnt plastic.

She sits and looks me over, sniffing again. "There were some anomalies during your examination," she begins.

"Anomalies...?" I ask, suddenly very glad that I am sitting down.

She licks my hand and my thrashing heart calms down to a fast beat.

"There were some polyps in your colon, one of them on the verge of being cancerous," she says. "But I took care of those. Nothing to worry about there."

Mia died of cancer so "nothing to worry about there" doesn't ring true to me.

Her nose twitches and she says, "Ashton Bach, you must trust me on this. Our medical technology is far more advanced than your ape technology."

"Okay..." I begin, trying to find words. "So you cured me of cancer and... there's something else...?" Without that magical doggy saliva a major freak out would have been on me by now for sure.

She licks my hand again and hops into my lap, her warm furry mass a comfort. I instinctively start to pet her and her tail gives a little wag.

"When we time jump," she begins, "I can see the planet shudder on the view screen. But it doesn't go out of focus and I certainly don't smell burning plastic or itch, nor does my stomach bother me."

"Okay..." I say, but this is feeling anything but.

"As you would expect, we scanned your brain during your examination," she says.

"Okay..." I say again. This seems to be the only word I have left anymore and my repeating it is kind of adding to the pending freak out, one bigger than the calming licks Angelica has delivered.

"Well, I might as well come out and say it," she says. "You

are an intelligent and capable ape, so I am sure that reason will prevail in your reaction."

"Okay..."

"The anomalies that concerned us were with your limbic lobe," she says. "Things were... well, they were a tad bit strange and we chalked it up to genetics, but now I must wonder if the time jumps are affecting you adversely."

And there it is. The reason we are sitting here in this forest in 2019 taking our time when not only do we have a mission, but Seattle is gone, and, presumably, humanity.

Thoughts of Mia vaporize and I feel panic settling in for a good long visit. "But... I... We...." I stammer. Well, at least I'm saying something besides "okay" over and over.

I take a deep breath and let it out, holding the corgi tightly to me. I take another deep breath and pretend I'm Samwise Gamgee, the loyal friend to Frodo Baggins, who faces the greatest terror imaginable to do the right thing and help his friend.

And Sam is a good model for me. I am not as smart as Angelica Huston and I am in a situation far past my ability to comprehend. But I can help. I can do something. I will be more than a middle-aged man freaking out about his inevitable mortality.

We all die. Every one of us. And she didn't even say this will kill me.

"Thank you for telling me, Angelica Huston," I say, remembering even in my state to use both her names. She is not Angelica or Angel or Ange. She is Angelica Huston, the corgi choosing her human name as tribute to the actress she loves so much.

"We have to do more time jumps," I add.

"Yes we do," she says.

"Let's get your ship back first," I say, giving her a little squeeze. "Then let's figure out what's going on with my limbic lobe."

"This is rational and wise, Ashton Bach," the corgi says in my mind and she nuzzles her face into my hand and I resume petting her.

And then something occurs to me. "But what about the double jump?"

"Are you sure about this?" she asks as she nuzzles me.

"Yes. Quite," I say. "The sequence happened twice, the second one was shorter, but otherwise it was the same."

I don't say anything about things going out of focus or itching or smelling burning plastic. That pending freak-out is restrained, so no reason to poke it.

Angelica lies down on my lap with a sigh and starts licking her paws. "That is not a good sign, Ash," she says. "The time-line is splitting and we must stop it."

CHAPTER TWENTY-SIX

BACK IN THE silver bone-shaped spaceship Angelica Huston brings up the time display.

I don't know what the official name of it is, but I remember it from our first adventure. The grainy black-and-white display shows threads weaving and dancing together forming a chaotic tapestry. Each thread is a being and it shows how they interact through time, how their paths are changed when they touch. The threads travel from the left side of the screen to the right.

Except the time display isn't a tapestry now. It's two threads which must be Angelica and me. But she winds it back, at least I think that is what she is doing as her paws twitch in the holes of her pedestal. She winds it back until our two threads disappear into a void and then on the other side come out of the kind of tangled tapestry I saw the first time.

"That is the jump," I mumble, mostly to myself. I'm leaning against the soft round wall of the bridge behind the corgi's low pedestal on the other side of the small room from the display. I can smell all the vague, complex smells that these canine ships always have. It's like I went and smelled too many spices and my nose is just on overload and can't pick out one scent from the next.

"Well done, Ash," Angelica says. "Now let's take a closer look."

The display is maddeningly black and white and so grainy, this technology clearly not created by beings with good eyesight or color perception, but it gets the job done.

The void is not empty as first I thought. It's not actually empty at all. It's chaos. All the threads enter it but two, Angelica and me, zoom off at a sharp angle, the tapestry of threads getting vaporous while our two threads get more solid and larger. Our two threads come out of the void, for the briefest moment, before entering another void. Except in this void, two other threads make a close pass to ours before our two threads go careening off and then finally exit the void to end up a tapestry of just two threads.

Where our threads diverge from the six, there is some kind of disturbance in the underlying darkness like rippling waves. It is what shoves us off course.

Angelica turns from the display and looks at me. "That was you, Ash, the future you. You knew where we would jump from and where we would jump to. You knocked us off course. It was well done, but a reckless act on your part."

"Off course..." I repeat, my brain trying to catch up.

"Yes indeed," she says. "We were knocked into a parallel timeline, one where you apes did not evolve."

"Can we get back?" I say.

The corgi pants briefly. "Yes. Because of your perception of the two jumps, I do have enough data to get us back. Our unplanned journey here has created a soft spot between our worlds. We must return quickly and properly so the damage to the space-time continuum can heal."

"Why is that a problem?" I ask.

The corgi looks around and sniffs the air at the stalk in front of her platform, her hackles raising. The display changes to the thick forest outside and I hear a roar, one that sends a shiver down my spine. It's definitely some kind of cat and not the kind that will be dissuaded by a squirt gun, even one spiked with habanero.

Yeah, okay, now I get why it would be a problem for there to be a soft spot between our world and this one.

"Are you sure you can repair the damage?" I ask, my heart thumping in my chest.

"Yes, Ashton Bach," she says. "I am very sure. We can fix this problem, but I don't know that it will do us any good back in our own timeline."

"Why?" I ask.

"Because, Ash. Your future-self knows every move we are going to make and doesn't want us to succeed."

CHAPTER TWENTY-SEVEN

I HAVE TO LAUGH. I'm not facing my evil twin from an alternate universe, I am facing my future-self that knows every move I am going to make because he already made it.

And these moves will turn me into him where I will thwart my past-self and do reckless things that damage the integrity of the timeline.

At the beginning of this, I had to wonder how I would turn into the person that would steal Angelica's spaceship, thinking it was just a scam, just me playing out the motions so the timeline remained healthy. That I would never really want to steal the ship and betray Angelica Huston.

I mean, to see Mia again, I can almost see it, but not quite. That's not who I am, but it is looking like that is who I will become.

As the spaceship lifts off, the grainy black-and-white display on the bridge shows us the creature we just heard. It's huge, a giant tiger that makes the tigers in our timeline look like house cats. It's all fangs and claws and dark vertical stripes. It leaps and suddenly grows large as the ship rises, giving us a fine view of its impressive fangs and its swiping claws.

Angelica barks and I cower against the soft curved wall of the bridge, my heart doing a fast tango in my chest.

The giant tiger falls back to the ground having missed us, but just. That tiger almost got itself a bone. That bone being a time-traveling spaceship with Angelica and me in it.

Which makes me wonder about my future-self, knocking us off course to such a dangerous place. But then again, he knew that we would lift off in time, that we would survive. He knows everything I'm going to do, so how can I defeat him?

It's a strange discussion to be having in your head, much less writing down. What can I possibly do that my future-self won't see coming?

Nothing.

Nothing at all.

I will allow that memory is imperfect, but these are the kinds of experiences that get burned into your brain. It's very unlikely that I will forget any of these moves. That I won't do everything I can to counter them so I can go see Mia.

Mia.

There is something there. Something tickling at the back of my mind again. I don't buy my own transformation into a ship-stealing, timeline-risking Angelica Huston-betraying person. There is something I don't know, something I don't understand that has to happen. Seeing Mia again is not quite enough to explain this.

I shake the thought off as the Earth falls below us, all

forest and plains and lakes with no signs of humanity. Even on the grainy black-and-white display, it is beautiful.

"I can't stop my future-self," I say, trying to get my brain back on track.

Angelica turns and looks at me. "I am sorry, Ash, but I must focus now. I do hope this isn't too unpleasant for you."

That's right. During my examination Angelica found anomalies with my limbic lobe. My experience of time jumping is not normal. Time jumps could be bad for me. They could be killing me.

I have to tell you when you're in the theater watching Sarah Conner fight for the future or Harry Potter facing Voldemort, it seems so exciting, so cool. But when you are in it, facing an enemy that seems unbeatable and worried about your own health, it's anything but.

Not cool and terrifying is a much better way to explain it than exciting.

I squeeze my eyes shut hoping that if I can't see the Earth stuttering and going out of focus, that I won't get super nauseous or get all itchy or smell burning plastic. Childish, yes, and at my age I should be far past childish, but I am not.

My eyes are closed for a while, it seems the setup for this maneuver is not an easy one. But it happens. I feel the shudder, my stomach flips, my skin gets hot and itchy, and I smell burning plastic. Not once, not twice, but three times.

When it's over and I open my eyes, the curve of the Earth is visible and I am gasping for breath.

Was this because it was a triple jump? Or because of my worry about my limbic lobe? Or is it getting worse, whatever is happening in my brain?

"Are you okay, Ashton Bach?" Angelica asks.

I do my best to smile and nod. "Did you repair the damage?" I ask.

She cocks her head. "Well, 'repair' is really the wrong word. I more cleaned the wound so it can heal."

"And do we need to worry about the soft spot?" I ask. "Will those creatures make their way to this timeline?" Visions of giant tigers rampaging through Seattle pass through my mind.

"Not unless they can make it into orbit," she says.

Of course. My imagination was getting away from me. The damage was where the ship jumped, not down on the surface. Well, one disaster averted.

"What do we do now, Ash?" Angelica asks.

And that is the question. Whatever it is, my future-self will know it and will do stupid and reckless things to stop us.

"I don't know," I say. "Maybe... maybe you should just take me home. Figure out a way to get your ship back without me. Any idea I come up with or any plan I am a part of my future-self will know."

The corgi is silent for a few breaths, her soulful brown eyes locked with mine. "But I do not understand you apes well enough to do this on my own," she finally says. "Your motivations, your rather primitive world view is something we struggle to understand. I am afraid I would be lost without your guidance."

And I'm not sure if Angelica implied this, but I certainly feel responsible for what my future-self has done. But I can't help. I can't plan. We need someone else.

I think of Jessica Cole, but she's retired and it's clear she knows quite a bit about all this. But that is her present-self, what about her past-self? After the battle with the cats in 1996 where Jessica was on their side, Angelica had me tell her to come back in a week. And Jessica had just told me, "And be gentle with my younger self when you meet her. She hasn't had good friends for as long as I have."

But Angelica was at Jessica's home when I found her, so they clearly have a relationship.

It hurts my brain, this time travel really does twist the tapestry that is all of us.

"Did you ever go back to 1996 and pick up Jessica?" I ask.

"No."

"Can you tell me how you knew where she was living in this time?" I ask. "What your history is with her?"

"It is best that I don't," she says. As I expected. Angelica's past-self has had interactions with the past Jessica, but she hasn't had any more interactions with the 1996 Jessica.

"Then that is it," I say. "We go get Jessica in 1996. She is smart and capable. We have her do the planning while I'm locked away somewhere and don't know what is going on."

As soon as I say it, I can see how desperate a plan it is. The 1996 Jessica held me at gunpoint to try to help the cats steal the ship. She was desperate to see her father again before he died—something I can relate to with Mia. This is not a person that can jump right in and help.

Not to mention that my future-self knows that we are going to recruit the 1996 Jessica Cole because this is my idea. We can expect resistance. We can expect a fight. But I don't see any way around it.

"Very well, Ash," Angelica says, her paws twitching in their holes as she turns towards the display.

"But do something unexpected," I say. "And don't tell me about it. I am going to close my eyes so I can't see where we land."

It's silly, really. I'm trying to hide information from my future-self by hiding it from myself. I am starting to really dislike the person that I become.

CHAPTER TWENTY-EIGHT

WE'RE in Seattle in a neighborhood I'm not going to describe very well because I can't. I have my eyes slitted and I'm staring at the corgi's tail as she trots down the sidewalk in front of me.

I suspect it's 1996, sometime a little before or a little after we told Jessica we would pick her up. But I don't know and that's the point.

I feel the damp air and hear the cars on the street as their tires hiss over the wet pavement. It's that Seattle kind of day when the air is so moist and the rain is so gentle that you can't really tell when it's raining and when it's not.

I've got my long black duster on keeping my body dry, but my hair is wet. My heart is beating hard and not from keeping up with Angelica, but because I fear my future-self is lurking, waiting for us, behind every corner, behind every tree. But I can't look up. I can't recognize anything. I just have to keep moving.

As much as I fear my future-self, I just want to have a conversation with him. Ask him why the hell he is doing this. Hope that he will listen to reason and we can stop all of this madness and go see Mia.

Or maybe he already has. Maybe that is what changed him. Jessica did say, "Sometimes the past is best left in the past." What did she mean by that?

So, you get the idea. I'm seeing as little as possible without falling on my face following the telepathic time-traveling corgi overthinking every little thing.

I don't know if you are like that, but I am. It's like my brain is kind of like a time-travel machine and it can take me to the past or the future at a whim where I can regret the past —missing Mia's rally, for example—or dreading the future— imagining the machinations of my sinister future-self.

We are at a door, a cracked cement sidewalk under my feet, and Angelica is barking. Loudly. Urgently. She hasn't said anything to me, so I don't look around, I just keep staring at her tail. The door is a deep purple and the bits of grass I can see on either side of the sidewalk look to be well tended.

I hear feet stomping towards us and feel a rush of air as the door opens. "What the hell is..." she begins, and I recognize the voice. It's a tad rough, like she smokes or used to smoke and more than a tad angry. Jessica Cole. "You're late," she says. I don't look up but can almost feel her glare on me. "And what's up with Rain Man here? Did you break him?"

ANGELICA IS TALKING to the 1996 Jessica Cole. She must be, because Jessica is rushing around closing drapes and turning off lights. I'm standing on a tile entryway, water slowly dripping off of me onto the floor, my sunglasses making the darkening room even darker.

"Come on," Jessica says after all that is done, gently taking my arm. I let her guide me through the house while my eyes are mostly squeezed shut. There could be so many clues. Pictures. A glimpse out the window. A unique article of clothing. Ignorance is the only weapon I have against my future-self and I'm going to use it.

The floor is wood with lots of throw rugs, I hear Angelica's nails clicking when we walk over the wood. We end up in the bathroom, more tile on the floor.

"Now open your damn eyes and tell me this is not complete insanity," Jessica says.

I sigh. We must seem insane, but I would think the telepathic corgi would sell it. "It is complete insanity," I say.

"Well what is this about the 'you that will be' that she's going on about?" Jessica asks nodding towards the corgi who is sitting next to me.

As I start to see more, I relax. The bathroom is a bathroom. The lights are off and in the dim illumination I can see a generic black-and-white picture of the Washington coast over the toilet, a metal shelf right under the mirror with a few toiletries neatly arranged, a blue shower curtain, and the toilet seat has one of those blue fuzzy things on it.

I take off my glasses and look at Jessica. She's tall, at around six feet she's almost as tall as me. Her bleach-blond hair is short, but not spikey this time, and she's not wearing any lipstick. She's wrapped in a threadbare black robe and looks entirely less intimidating than the other two times I've seen her.

But my mouth is still sore from when she punched me so I am still wary.

I sigh. How the hell do you explain this stuff with clarity and efficiency. And it's not as if the content of what I have to say is benign, it's embarrassing as hell. So I just say it.

"Ahh... A future version of me is working with the cats and has stolen Angelica Huston's spaceship. He knows every move we're going to make because he used to be me. We need your help getting the spaceship back. You are our only hope."

Her blue eyes are darting from my face down to the corgi and back. Her brow furrows and her mouth moves a bit before she turns to Angelica and speaks. "I waited for you," she says. "I slunk to that yard day after day and you never showed up."

"That's my fault," I say. "We couldn't come on that day or my future-self would know where we would be."

She ignores me and is staring at the corgi, her arms crossed.

"I am sorry for that, Jessica Cole," I hear Angelica say in my head. But it's different, her voice is not quieter, but less intense. I know she's not talking to me. "But given our first encounter and how you tried to steal the ship, I think your indignation is a bit overwrought."

"It's not like I stole your ship, though," she says. "It's this Einstein that did that to you." She rubs at her face. "Or *will* do that to you."

"Will you help us?" I ask.

"Will she take me to see my father?" Jessica asks, her arms still crossed. "First. Before we go gallivanting off after this evil future you."

She stares at me and then at the corgi and all the clues of her appearance sink in. She's depressed. She's been isolating herself since Angelica didn't show up. She's got something around her father like I have around Mia.

"We can't do that, Ash," Angelica says in my head and I get the impression she is only talking to me. Now that's convenient. "We must get my ship back first and return this version of the ship to the me that was."

"Why do you need to see your father so badly?" I ask Jessica.

She blinks, her hard blue eyes darting away. There is something there. The future Jessica told me that this version of her didn't have good friends, and from older Jessica's greeting it looks like we became friends and more. Which is so distracting. This version of Jessica is younger than me (and fitter and stronger), so the part of me that is slave to the evolutionary imperative to reproduce notices the curves beneath her robe even in her depressed state.

But I shake that off. "My wife, Mia, she died of cancer," I begin with a sigh. "I was with her every day, every doctor's appointment, for the whole damn fight all the way until it was clear the fight couldn't be won and she entered hospice."

Jessica is looking at me now, her eyes not nearly as hard.

"I lost it on her last day," I say. "Her breath was rattling as her lungs filled up with fluid. The sound grew to be like fingernails on a chalkboard. I lost it. I walked out and got in my car and drove. While I was gone, she rallied, she talked to her parents and her brother. They got to say their goodbyes. Her last goodbyes. She was in a coma by the time I got word of her rally and could get back."

The room feels small and I am sweating, the panting of the corgi seeming loud.

Jessica's eyes narrow and her lips purse. "And this is why you will steal her spaceship?"

I shrug. "It's the only reason I can think of. To be there with her at the end. To tell her that I love her one more time. I loved her with all my heart and I missed my last chance to say goodbye." I shrug again. If that doesn't make sense, I don't know what will.

In the dim light, I can see tears forming in her eyes, but then her face hardens. "Get out," she says, nodding toward the door. "Both of you get the hell out of my home and find some other sucker."

"Wait. What?" I ask.

"Don't you see?" she asks, nodding down at Angelica. "This little beast here will never let you go back to that time, will never let you say goodbye to your wife."

"What the hell are you talking about?" I look at Angelica, but the dog is looking away. "What is she talking about?"

"Think it through, Einstein," Jessica says. "If she would give you that one thing, that one small thing, there'd be no reason for you to go rogue in the future. You'd say your tearful goodbye, feel a hell of a lot better about yourself, and wouldn't team up with her enemies to steal the ship."

Angelica isn't talking, in fact, she's standing up and facing the door like a domesticated dog that needs to go relieve itself.

"And if she won't do that for you, how can I know that she will let me see my father," Jessica says, her voice rising in volume. "Come see me after you've stolen the ship, but for now get the hell out of my apartment!"

CHAPTER TWENTY-NINE

THE DOOR SLAMS and we're back out in the moist air, my legs so weak I just sink onto the wet step. What the hell am I doing? If Angelica won't help me then I should be helping my future-self, not trying to stop him.

Is this the piece that was missing, the thing that I couldn't see that turns me into the man that would join with the cats and steal Angelica's spaceship?

"Ashton Bach," she begins in my head. "If you will but listen, I can explain." She's sitting there and I can smell that comforting wet dog smell, but it is at odds with what I am feeling.

"You're not going to let me see her," I say. It's not a question.

"I cannot," she says, emotion bleeding through her cultured English accent.

She's got those deep brown eyes trained on me, like she

can see into my soul and I want to look away, but I can't. "Why?"

The corgi sighs in my head and says, "This is a difficult thing to convey, I—"

"Right. Right," I say, cutting her off. "My inferior ape brain and the complexities of time travel. Blah, blah, blah."

"No, Ashton Bach," she says. "That is not it. Not at all. If you go back, if you see your wife and say your last goodbyes, it will..." The corgi looks away out to the misty neighborhood and I miss her soulful eyes.

"It will damage you," she says.

"Damage me?" I ask. "How? I mean, I know it will be hard, so hard, but how can it hurt me to have one more precious moment with the woman I love?"

Despite the cool weather, Angelica pants a bit and then says, "I do not understand this part," she says. "But we did this before. I took you to see her, to right that wrong, and..."

"And what?" I ask, my mind spinning. I've seen Mia on her death bed during her rally? We did this before?

"I can only show you," she says and trots off.

BY THE TIME we get back to Angelica Huston's bone-shaped time-traveling spaceship, I'm desperate. Desperate to know what happened when Angelica took me to see Mia "before." Desperate to know how all this time-travel stuff works, because I don't remember this. And even more desperate to see Mia.

It's almost like I can feel myself changing into my "evil"

future-self. Like it's not so surprising anymore that I would team up with the cats to steal Angelica's ship. It makes sense that I would do this to a past version of her so she wouldn't see it coming. That I would do it to defy whatever she is going to show me, prove that it doesn't have to be that way.

That's my brain. Time traveling ahead and envisioning what might be before I even have half a clue.

On the bridge of the ship, Angelica gets on the small pedestal and inserts her paws. The curved display on the wall of the bridge comes to life, but this time it's not showing the planet or the time tapestry, but a grainy video of this very bridge.

I'm overwhelmed with strong scents as the canine technology communicates olfactory information from the recording. It's strong enough to overpower the damp smell of the corgi and me and I smell sweat, sharp and fearful. There are other scents, but they are too complex for my nose to make them out.

The video shows me. I don't have my Neo-style duster on but a sweater and jeans. I'm curled up in the fetal position weeping while Angelica licks at my face and I bat her away. I am rocking and say "Mia, Mia, Mia. My Mia." I punch the soft floor and kick out with my leg.

The display goes blank and the scents recede and I'm left there with my stomach tight and my hands shaking.

"You need to explain this," I say, my voice sounding distant.

"I am sorry, Ashton Bach," she says, "but I don't know if I can."

"My name is Ash," I growl. I had noticed that the corgi

uses my full name when she is stressed and my nickname when she is calm. This tells me something about the canines, that using a being's full name is natural for them. First names and nicknames are not, so when she is stressed she falls back to using my full name.

While a dim part of me is fascinated by it, that is only a dim part. I am angry at Angelica for not taking me right to see Mia, for showing me this tiny blip of a video and somehow expecting it to be enough, for calling me by my full name.

Interspecies relationships can be hard and I am in a space where I am the one making it hard.

"I am sorry, Ash," she says meekly in my head. "I cannot explain your reaction because I do not understand it."

"Well then," I say, hugging my knees to my chest in the cramped space. "Tell me everything you know. Tell me when this happened and if it will happen again."

The corgi pulls her paws out of their holes and hops off the low pedestal and sits on the other side of the bridge from me, her radar ears seeming more at attention than usual. "The last part is easier to answer," she says. "It will never happen again and it was a mistake that it happened in the first place. As I told you when we met, you were my first time-travel mission, but what you remember is not the first time we met, not the first time we time traveled back to see your Mia."

CHAPTER THIRTY

TIME TRAVEL IS NOT for the faint of heart or for those that cannot tolerate paradox or twisting timelines. And I am beginning to think that it is not for me.

I'm not a Rose Tyler or Amy Pond, capable companions to Doctor Who. I'm not even a Marty McFly. I'm Ashton Bach, computer programmer, sci-fi geek, and widower. Angelica Huston should have let me be, left me in my apartment on my nice quiet Saturday, programming away, doing my job as a bit slinger for hire. Not taken me the first time, right to Mia so I could be with her during her rally, and not the second time when we skipped through her young life and I got to act like a guardian angel for her.

"That first time is gone," she says on the other side of the bridge from me, her head down, her fur damp and bedraggled. "It is locked away in a bubble of time. I went back a little earlier and got you for the second time and I did it quickly enough so that this timeline just closed in around my mistake and this version of it took hold."

I'm silent, trying to process it all. I saw Mia during her rally and it was devastating. Well... of course it was. Me two years distant from her death going back and experiencing it again... yeah, that would be devastating. Terrible. But wonderful in some ways too.

Mia and I were together for twenty years. I loved her from her youth into middle age. I loved her healthy and I loved her sick. Surely I could love her during her last lucid moments.

"I need to understand why it did that to me," I say, my teeth almost grinding together.

The corgi lowers her head farther. "There is more to the recording, but I do not believe it is a good idea, Ashton Ba... Ash."

"I need to understand this," I say.

The corgi doesn't move. And from where I am sitting now, I understand her reticence. Just as I could feel me changing, she could feel me changing. I was becoming the man that would steal her spaceship and I hadn't helped her get it back first.

"Please," I say. "Please, Angelica Huston. I must understand this."

She gives a slight whimper but slowly gets on the pedestal and puts her paws in. The grainy black-and-white display shows me in fetal position, dressed in jeans and a sweater, mumbling Mia's name over and over again.

My stomach tightens like a vice grip and I want to run away. I have been like that before, after Mia died, after there was no more battle to fight or vigil to hold. After the funeral home had come taken her body away and after everyone else had left. I collapsed on the floor and cried her name out like that. For a long time. For how long, I can't say.

"Why?" the me on the screen says. "Why did you do this to me?"

"I am so sorry, Ashton Bach," the corgi on the screen says. "I thought this is what you wanted." I can actually hear Angelica's voice through my ears and not just in my head. Somehow the technology these canines have can record their telepathic speech.

"How could I know," the grieving me on the screen says.

"What happened?" the corgi asks gently as she backs away from my thrashing legs. "Can you explain it to me, Ashton Bach?"

I see me punch the floor some more, and while I'm speaking, none of the words are intelligible.

This is so hard to write about. The me on the grainy black-and-white screen is me, but it's not the me that I am now. This particular feeling isn't just a byproduct of time travel, it's a byproduct of time. The passage of time dulls our empathy for ourselves. I know some of the stupid things I did in my twenties and I can't imagine how I ever did those things because I am not that person anymore.

And more so, because of time travel, I don't fully relate to that person that is on the screen, because even though he is quite literally me, this experience is not one that I've had.

"She knew," the me on the screen says. "And she was scared."

"What do you mean?" the corgi on the screen asks.

On the screen, I stop with the trashing and slowly sit up

wiping the snot off my nose with my sweater. "She knew," I say, my voice raw and stretched like it's about to break. "She knew."

"What did she know?" the corgi on the screen asks.

"She knew I didn't belong there. She didn't want me there. She was afraid of me."

Sitting there watching this, I draw my knees closer as my hands tremble. The me on the screen isn't making perfect sense, but a picture is forming in my brain.

"Please, Ashton Bach," Angelica says on the screen. "I do not understand. What went wrong?"

"I scared her," I hiss on the screen. "She was terrified. She knew I didn't belong there. She thought I was the devil come to take her soul. She died. She died in terror."

"Enough!" I shout from my sitting position. "Turn it off. Please turn it off."

Angelica hops onto the pedestal and the video stops and all that is there is the curved grey wall. My heart is galloping in my chest and I am having trouble breathing.

I know what happened and I was wrong about why I stole Angelica's ship—or rather why I *will* steal Angelica's ship. It makes perfect sense. And I have to do it. I have to steal her ship and do a whole lot more. I have to make this all work out. But how?

CHAPTER THIRTY-ONE

ON THE BRIDGE of her spaceship, as I lean against the soft curved wall, Angelica Huston is licking my hand tentatively. It seems that watching the past-me, the one locked away in the time bubble, rattled her too. She's afraid of me now and acting like a stray that is not sure the human she found will be kind or will be cruel.

I feel a touch of calmness from Angelica's magical doggy licks, but I beat it back. I can't be calm right now. I need to think. I need to plan. I need to figure out what lie I need to tell the corgi so I can make this all work.

That evil-self that I thought was coming is here. And, not surprisingly, I don't think I am evil and I am very sure the me that I was before I saw that video was quite naïve. Ridiculously so.

We apes are an optimistic lot most of the time. I think it's required for survival. And I was being overly optimistic about seeing Mia again, thinking it would be so good for me and so good for her. But it was a selfish thought. The first part was probable (it being good for me) the last part was a hopeful rationalization (it being good for her).

Here's what I think happened.

No. Wait. First a little precursor. You need some context to understand this.

When it comes to religion and the afterlife, I am not religious nor am I an atheist. My view can be succinctly summoned up as "I have no freaking clue." Seriously. I don't. I think I understand human nature enough to really get why the belief in God can be comforting and can even help us be better humans. But also know that what we really want to be true, often isn't. We are really good at fooling ourselves.

And then on the other hand I am well aware that we barely understand this world we live in (there are telepathic time-traveling canines and felines, as case in point).

So here's what I think happened.

One. Mia in her halfway across the veil state recognized something different in me, that I didn't belong there.

Two. Her latent religious training came to bear and combined with her strange dying biochemistry, she thought I was some manifestation of the Grim Reaper.

Three. (And this is the tough one.) Mia didn't want me there for her last rally. She couldn't bear to say that final goodbye to me. After I walked out, some part of her knew I was gone, and she rallied and was able to have closure with her family. To have the closure she could bear to have.

Yeah. It's a hell of a thing. I could be wrong, this could be my sci-fi geek immersion spinning out an entertaining story.

See the part about "we are really good at fooling ourselves" above. What I do know is that the time-bubble me had a terrible experience and so did Mia. And that is what I have to stop.

I have to stop all of this. And I know how... at least I think I do. I have the bare outline of a plan in my head. I know there are a lot of missing details, but it's at the stage where it's more hope than reality, but I need hope.

"I'm okay," I say to the now shy corgi and gently pet her. "It is good that you showed me that, Angelica Huston. I know how to make this right."

The corgi sits and levels those soulful brown eyes at me and I want to tell her everything but I can't. I have to make this work. "I am so very glad to hear you say that, Ashton Bach," she says in my head. "How do we make this right?"

I do my best to smile, but it feels like a bitter thing. "I need you to trust me," I say, a plan coalescing my brain. Not quite a plan, really, but an outline, a beautiful possibility. "Is there a way I can do some time jumps without you?"

Angelica cocks her head and stares at me for a moment and then turns her head and looks at the low pedestal. "Well, Ash. I can program some sequences simple enough for you to trigger with your ape fingers. It won't be easy, but I think you are up to it."

I nod my head but then frown. "But I will have a past version of the ship. How will that work?" I ask.

"It's a time drive, Ash," she says. "Past and future are the same to it."

Clearly my ape brain won't ever truly grasp this time-travel stuff, but at least it will work. "It's going to be all right,"

I say. "I promise. You'll get your ship back for sure and no one will ever have to know."

I'm telling her the truth, but not all the truth. And that's how I know that I'm not Ashton Bach anymore. I'm really Ash now. I'm about to earn that name.

PART THREE

EVIL ASH THE TIME TRAVELER

CHAPTER THIRTY-TWO

I WAS OBSESSED with Möbius strips when I was a kid. You take a strip of paper, twist it once, and then tape it into a circle. Then run your finger along one side of the paper and before you know it your finger is on the other side of the paper. You have created a one-sided object with just a twist and a little scotch tape.

If you are being technical, a Möbius strip is a one-sided non-orientable surface. I am coming to think of time travel like that. One sided and, especially, non-orientable. In mathematical terms, orientability has a very specific meaning that is a bit beyond me as a bit slinger, but in terms of this story I am telling you and time travel, it's what it sounds like. With the past and the present and the future all being mixed up like this, there is no orienting. Not really. Our ape minds are not built for it.

But then there is sci-fi to the rescue and I have lots of

examples to pull from to try to understand all of this. None that quite cover this, but close enough.

I'm thinking about the Möbius strip as I stand in front of Jessica Cole's purple apartment door in 1996. Angelica Huston and I have finished our preparations and she's waiting in the ship while I take care of this bit of prep. I need to make a Möbius strip out of Jessica and me.

"Hey, Rain Man," she says when she yanks the door open. "What do you want? Where's your better half?"

I'm not restricting my vision or trying to hide information from my "evil" future-self. I am him. There is no reason.

She's still in her robe, no makeup, her short bleach-blond hair flat and lifeless. The neighborhood is a nice one, her building made of red brick with cheerful flower beds out front. The mist has receded and the day is damp and cool but not so wet anymore.

"I have a favor to ask you," I say.

She crosses her arms in front of her and her full lips quirk into a half-smile. "Really?"

I nod.

"Is it the pleasure of taking me to see my father?" she asks.

I shake my head. "Someone a lot smarter than me once told me that sometimes the past is best left in the past."

Her brow furrows and her blue eyes narrow. "What the hell happened to you, Rain Man?"

"The name is Ash," I say, and a dim part of me notices that I say it with no hesitation or embarrassment whatsoever. "Can I come in? This won't take very long."

I can see the curiosity in her eyes as she looks me up and down. I'm still wearing the long black duster, but I feel different in it now. It doesn't feel like a costume anymore. It feels like me. Like Ash.

"Why not?" she says with a shrug, waving me into her home with an exaggerated flourish.

The living room is sparse and neat. Colorful rugs mostly hiding the scarred hardwood floors. The furniture all has touches of blond wood with simple cushions in bright colors. The art on the walls tends towards watercolor depicting outdoor scenes, places of beauty. There is no TV but an over-flowing bookshelf, the only thing in the room that isn't very neat.

I hesitate. What I have to tell her is... well, it's tricky and I realize I don't actually know anything about her. I know she can handle a gun and knows how to throw a punch. I know she likes gardening (or will like gardening). And I know she was desperate enough to see her father to team up with alien cats.

"So?" she asks, her arms crossed and her hip cocked.

She's beautiful even in her depressed frumpy stage. Nothing like Mia who was slim and dark. Jessica is tall and curvy and combative and strong. It occurs to me that there is an easy way to do this. I can promise her what she wants not knowing if it will happen to get what I want. But I'm not that person and hopefully I won't become that person.

"You know what a Möbius strip is?" I ask.

She nods. "One-sided thingamabob some German dude came up with about 150 years ago. What does this have to do with anything?"

"You and me," I say, deciding to go with the truth. "I want

to turn my last day and the ways we interacted into a Möbius strip."

"Your last day?" she asks, and I have to smile. I didn't say "the" last day but "my" last day.

"Yeah," I say. "It started in 2019 with you kissing me."

She blinks and her mouth moves and I almost laugh seeing her at a loss for words, but she recovers quickly. "And... that stupid line is somehow supposed to let you kiss me now? Because, you know, I'd be very happy to punch you again."

"No," I say, feeling my cheeks flush red. "I need to tell you what happened in 2019 so it can happen again."

She's silent for a couple of breaths. "I think I need some whiskey. You?"

"Yes, please," I say.

She comes back with two crystal glasses with two fingers of the amber liquid, the pungent smell of it calling to me. She gives me one, hastily clinks her glass to mine and shoots it back. I take a small sip not wanting to have a coughing fit like I did with the future Jessica.

"Lay it on me, Ash," she says with a smile that seems half playful and half ironic. She flops into an armchair and motions me to sit on the couch.

So I sit down and tell her. In detail. Not everything but how she spooked me with intimacy, how she called me "babe" and seemed to really know me. How she kissed me and slapped me on the ass.

"Just to be clear," she says when I'm done. "You are not asking to practice these things right now."

"No," I say, shaking my head.

"I take it I'm still pretty hot in my sixties."

"Yes," I say.

She leans back, her arms crossed, and just stares at me. I'm leaning forward on the couch, actually I think it's a futon and can become a bed, and take another sip of whiskey.

"You're afraid of it," she finally says. "That's why you're here."

"What?" I ask. I have no idea what she is talking about.

"You're afraid of something real happening between us," she says. "And I'll grant you that it's a hell of a long shot, but you come here, you don't offer to give me what I want, but you ask me to do all these things when we meet in twenty-three years."

"Okay..." I say. I'm still not getting it.

"This Möbius strip of us you are trying to make," she says with a sigh. "It's so you can walk away from here assured that we didn't really have a relationship. That the old me just did what you asked her to. You're afraid."

My heart is thudding in my head and I don't think it's the little bit of whiskey I've drunk. She's right that I'm afraid, but wrong about the scope of what I'm afraid of. It's not just a relationship with her that has me scared.

I give her a small nod and sip more of the whiskey.

"What's in it for me?" she asks.

I look up at her surprised. I shouldn't be, but I am.

"I don't get to see my father," she begins, her blue eyes icy. "I don't get to go time traveling. I just have to remember to kiss you twenty-some years from now and slap your skinny ass. So what's in it for me?"

My mouth moves and I fear I've made a terrible mistake. The future Jessica Cole is very different from this woman.

She laughs, it's loud and fills the room. "Can you at least give me a good stock tip?"

I blink. Can I? Would I be harming anything? Is this what I always do when time twists around and Jessica and I are here.

"Umm... Apple and Amazon. Those our good bets," I say.

She smiles and her brow briefly furrows like she's reevaluating me.

"We have a deal then," she says and extends her hand. "Provided those stocks work out, I'll do what you say when we meet in 2019. When you look like this with that pretty little bruise on your cheek."

The bruise that she gave me.

It's clear I should go, and as I stand up, I don't feel the relief I had hoped to feel.

"You know," she begins from her chair. "Just because you made a Möbius strip out of this day of yours doesn't mean something doesn't happen between us."

Her laughter rings out as I let myself out of her apartment. I'm not sure if I like that thought or hate it.

CHAPTER THIRTY-THREE

WHEN ANGELICA HUSTON and I travel to 2019, as the Earth stutters and goes out of focus, as the nausea and itching hits me like a wave and I smell burning plastic, I only think of my limbic lobe briefly. It's an afterthought now, the anomaly Angelica Huston saw there, the damage that may or may not be happening with each jump, isn't a worry anymore.

I know how to take care of that. I know how to do everything. Well... kind of.

Excuse me while I wax poetic—I hope—about software for a moment. I've experienced this many times. As I design a solution there is a moment when I can feel it, I know it is there, I know there is an elegant way to solve the problem but I don't exactly know all the little details. What I'm trying to do with this time-traveling mess I am in is like that. I can feel it, I know it's possible, even though I don't know all the details yet.

On the bridge, we are both silent as the grainy black-and-white display shows Seattle coming into view once again. The jumps I need are programmed into the ship and I know how to trigger them. Jessica Cole has her stock tips and will greet me in 2019 just the right way. Angelica Huston has spent the time and explained to me a bit more about how time travel works. How the timeline resists splitting off parallel universes, and time bubbles are created as a way for it to heal itself, like a tree forming a burl to heal from a wound.

I am one of those people who only very rarely feels sure of themselves. This is one of those times. What I need to do is so clear and I have no doubts.

That should have been my first sign that I was in over my head.

In the thick forest of Interlaken Park after Angelica has let me out of the spaceship, I pause. I can feel the corgi's brown eyes on my back. I can feel her questions without her asking them.

I have asked a lot of her. I convinced her to program in jumps for me that didn't make sense to her.

"I'm going to take care of this, Angelica Huston," I say, my back to her, the air damp and full of birdsong. The blue sky above is bright and it's warm in my duster. "I'm going to steal your ship right when I need to and I'll have a bunch of cats with me. This will work. I promise."

"Are you quite sure, Ash?" she asks.

I turn around and manage a smile. "Yes. I am quite sure. I know what needs to be done. When you return the ship to Colorado, be sure it's in a slightly different position."

"Of course," she says. It's time travel 101. She needs her past-self to experience the ship being slightly moved so this can all happen again, another Möbius strip of causality.

And I need to betray her and steal her ship just like I already did. Her past, my future.

"Thank you for trusting me," I say.

"You are a good ape," she replies.

I walk away and don't look back. The next time I see Angelica Huston, I'll be stealing her ship. But first I have some preparations to make.

IT FEELS good to be back in my own time, but it's a day before I flew up here looking for Jessica Cole trying to find the time-traveling corgi.

Timing is very important in time travel (duh). I've got to steal the ship in time for Angelica Huston to be forlorn in the backyard of Jessica Cole's house before the past-me gets up here looking to hitch a ride to go back in time to see Mia.

Another twisting Möbius strip of causality. I have found that I can't think about it too much or I get a headache.

I walk to the edge of the park, get an Uber, and have it take me to a toy store, a pet store, and then to a hardware store. There is some theater that has to happen here, and I need props.

Angelica called this few days here a "nexus." There is a lot of time traveling going on, her silver bone-shaped spaceship traveling to and from these few days in Seattle over and over. She asked me to be careful, that the nexus has softened the time space continuum a bit, that bad things can happen.

But bad things have happened, will happen again, and it

all seems to revolve around me. And Mia. And my desire to see her again, to right the wrong of me missing her rally.

Which doesn't seem so wrong anymore. But how can something like that be relative, be a matter of perspective? That video I saw of me, the time-bubble me, explaining what happened when I went back to right that wrong is haunting. It's like it's a companion, a presence, a guide as I try to sort this out. I don't want to do that to Mia. I don't want to do that to me.

But it happened. And as I understand the rules of time travel, there is no undoing it, but there is something I can do. I can restore me, the Ashton Bach that existed before all this happened.

This may be hard to understand, why a geek like me would want to go back to being Ashton Bach? But think of it this way. Before Angelica Huston I was a lonely widow, but healing. Now the wound has been ripped open and all I can think of is Mia. I just don't think I can live like this.

I have the Uber take me to nearby Washington Park and I wander through the paths beneath the tall trees until I'm not sure where I am. Washington Park is vast with paved trails, mowed grass, and an arboretum. The sunshine has made it muggy and I find a secluded spot in the shade of the trees and take off my duster and lay it down on the ground and sit on it. I open the packages, get out my tools, and go to work.

I take parts from a couple ultrasonic bark deterrents, LEDs and switches from a silly dancing robot, and a few other cheap toys. I take them all apart, use my reading glasses so I can see things close up, and reassemble them into something that looks... well, I want to say it looks formidable, but it's a plastic contraption with LEDs and buttons that looks more Frankensteinish than anything. It's got grey plastic, black plastic, three different button types, all glued and taped together, but it will do the trick.

I went to college to become a bit slinger and took some electrical engineering courses. I know how to use a soldering iron (I got a little battery-powered one from the hardware store) and I know how to put in switches and wire up power.

It's not rocket science... or maybe I should say it's not time-travel science, but it will do for what I need. It fits nicely in my hand and is roughly rectangular, three big push button switches in easy reach of my thumb.

I also take some cheap work gloves and add in a switch, a battery, and LED lights along the fingertips. It doesn't actually do anything besides light up, but I'm hoping it's enough to fool some cats.

I clean up carefully, getting all the packaging and discarded pieces of plastic and unused electronics and bag them up.

It's time to find some telepathic alien felines and steal a spaceship.

As I get up and put on my duster, I feel it. I am Ash. I am that "evil" version of myself that I was fearing. But I have to say that Ashton Bach would be enjoying this all a lot more than Ash is.

Ashton would be full of wonder whereas I am grimly determined. Ashton would be cataloging how the fiction he loves so much aligns with his current adventure whereas I am focused on getting this right.

I kind of miss Ashton.

CHAPTER THIRTY-FOUR

THIS IS THE HARD PART. Finding the cats.

It was back in 1984 through 1996 that Angelica and I fought off the pack of cats led by the big black one. That was twenty-three years ago, that cat can't possibly be alive, can it?

But when I asked Angelica Huston about our canine companions in comparison to her kind, she told me they were the same race, she said, "They accepted a greatly shortened life and blocked off the most powerful parts of their minds so they could be of service to you apes."

Could that be true for cats? I mean for dogs, I get it. Police dogs, seeing eye dogs, drug sniffing dogs, dog sleds. Dogs contribute to our society. Dogs are clearly in service. But cats?

This is a blind spot for me. I am not a cat person. I don't have anything in particular against them (although we all now know why every cat in the world hates me) but I do not see them ever being labeled as a "service animal." A "comfort animal," certainly, so maybe it is the same. Maybe cats are in service to humanity. Or maybe humanity is in service to cats.

Don't get me wrong, that last part is a good thing. I think what is so good about animals for so many people is that it forces us to think about another being first. Gets us out of bed on the days we don't want to. Makes us constantly be aware of another entity's needs. This fights what appears to be our inherent apish selfishness and narcissism.

This day, though, as I walk out of Washington Park, the sun blazing and the air muggy, none of that matters. Finding alien telepathic cats is what matters. Could that big black cat still be alive? It had looked older the last time I saw it, but this is time travel, so who knows.

My intent with the cats is not honorable. I am not interested in what they want, I am not here to serve them. I need to use them for theatrical purposes to set up what will happen and what has already happened from Angelica's perspective. To set up what will happen from both of our perspectives.

With my new cobbled together, time-traveler's theatrical gizmos in my duster pocket, I call another Uber and start looking for cats.

Doctor Who has his sonic screwdriver that can do many magical things with technology, and I have my ultrasonic gizmo. It is sadly limited compared to the Doctor's screwdriver, but I smile as I'm driven through the unusually sunny streets of Seattle. There is still the geeky Ashton in me and that gives me hope.

All this time I longed to become Ash and now I miss Ashton.

The Uber takes me to the same neighborhood I last saw

the big black cat back in 1996 and drops me off at the bar where I met Mia.

As the car pulls away, I stare at the building. I'm in an older part of town and this century-old brick building used to be some kind of factory, and then it was split up into trendy retail in the nineties, and now it is abandoned with boarded up windows and weeds invading the sidewalk. It looks oddly dour in the bright sunlight, as if it longs for the clouds and the mists to hide it from the world.

This is where the young me met Mia. This is where I met Jessica Cole just a few days ago subjectively. For me this is the nexus of all this time travel.

I have no clue if I will find any alien telepathic cats here, but I couldn't think of anywhere else to go. And I kind of feel fate pulling me along. This has happened before. It will happen again.

That thought is Ash not Ashton. I mean, Ashton would understand the concept, the Möbius strip of causality we are working on, but he wouldn't feel confident about it. Ash is confident. I am confident.

I don't go into the old two-story building. I don't want to see what has become of that bar. I don't want to see it in ruin and disrepair. I don't want to think too much about what I am doing and what it will mean to me, to what happened in this place.

I walk quickly down the sidewalk, turn down an alley, and head towards the back of the building, my hands reaching into my duster pockets. I have no clue what is going to happen, but this is now the kind of neighborhood where you want to keep your weapons close. And, yes, an ultrasonic gizmo in one pocket is nearly useless in most conventional situations as is the habanero-spiked squirt gun in the other, but my life has been far from conventional lately.

In back of the building there is nothing but weeds and cracked blacktop and more broken windows. Doubt starts to creep in, but I push it down. What did I think? That the cats would be haunting this area for decades waiting for me to return and offer them what they wanted so desperately the last time we met?

I kick at the dead leaves on the blacktop and pace in a circle around the parking area. Since I know the future-me solved this problem (the past Angelica Huston interacted with that me) then I know the problem is solvable. But I don't know that it's easy to solve. But, on the other hand, I do know there is a limited amount of time to solve the problem. Angelica told me the time and place that the future me stole her spaceship and that gives me about twenty-four hours to find the cats, convince them that I am going to help them, and execute the plan.

I speed up my pacing and think. There has to be a solution because there was a solution. I did this before so I will do it again.

This is why it's not a good idea to know the future, it puts you in this weird place. Like, I am confident I will find the cats which seems to be messing with my ability to actually find the cats. The problem has been solved by my future-self which is disincentivizing my current-self.

Is the journey worth taking if you know exactly how it's going to turn out?

Except I don't know. I do know I'll steal the ship. What comes after that is only a hope.

And that jogs my brain and I start really thinking. If there are telepathic alien cats in Seattle, where would they be? What would they be doing? Would it be more than lounging in the sun and letting their apes take care of them?

In my previous adventure skipping through time helping out the younger Mia, the cats always seemed to know where Angelica's spaceship would be.

We never saw them at Interlaken Park, but there might be a good reason for that. The first time Angelica and I were beamed up into the larger ship and earlier today the ship was only there briefly. But before, when the ship was on the ground for a while, the cats always found it.

Which means they had technology or knowledge that told them where Angelica would be touching down. Which means they might know where she is landing in twenty-four hours. Which means I know where they will be in twenty-four hours. Maybe I'm not the one to bring them there, maybe they will already be there.

I pull out my phone and request another Uber.

CHAPTER THIRTY-FIVE

THE ALIEN CANINES have what seems to be a database of vacant houses. When we were interacting with the young Mia, it was always some overgrown backyard we were landing the spaceship in. And now, as I go seeking the cats, it is another vacant house, this one with a "For Sale" sign out front.

I am back near Washington Park in a neighborhood called Madison Valley. It's a lovely older Seattle neighborhood with lots of trees, older houses, and narrow sloping streets with sidewalks on both sides.

Mia and I didn't live here, too expensive for us because of its proximity to downtown, but it reminds me of our neighborhood and that is hard.

After seeing the video of my time-bubble self, after he saw Mia during her rally, I feel this growing void threatening me. I had two years to grieve her loss and then Angelica Huston came and took me skipping through her young life and I began to hope that I could see her one more time.

And now I know I can't. Ever. For any reason.

My hope has twisted into despair and that is why I am doing this.

Angelica didn't give me an exact address of this house. It's not how they organize things in their canine database. She started out telling me all about how it smelled but that doesn't work for my poor ape olfactory system.

She ended up saying it was white and narrow with distinctive windows with one pane of glass making up the bottom three-quarters of the window and a series of smaller panes making up the top of the window. She also said that the front yard was mostly concrete with tiered flower beds.

It took me some time, but I found it. And the "For Sale" sign really helped. The house was old but had clearly been remodeled, everything excessively neat and orderly.

It was the middle of the day on a work week and I didn't hesitate. I walked around the side of the house and climbed the stairs and slipped through the wooden gate into the fenced backyard.

There were towering pine trees there with just enough room for Angelica's spaceship to land, but there were no cats.

They will be here sometime before Angelica. And then it hits me—she didn't tell me when the future-me, the almost here me, stole the spaceship (will steal the spaceship... damn verbs). And thinking about it, I was fixated on finding the cats before Angelica got here, but what we saw before was the cats would find the ship after it landed. It was when we were coming back after doing a mission that they would be there. Almost like they had some kind of technology to detect the canine ship after it had arrived.

And that must be the case now. I need to be here when the cats get here which will be after Angelica Huston lands. Then I'll have to find a way to steal the ship when the corgi comes back. As usual with this time-travel stuff, I'm a little short on details.

There are a few hotels on Madison near downtown, which isn't that far. So, I leave the house, walk out of the neighborhood, and head down Madison.

It's a rare sunny day in Seattle and I enjoy the moment.

Madison is a busy street, it runs at a diagonal across the orderly north-south and east-west streets, cutting through the city. Despite its busyness it's only two lanes here, and my path is shaded by towering trees and cuts through this eclectic older Seattle neighborhood.

It's hot, but it's also humid, so it in no way feels like Phoenix and that feels good.

I spot a few cats and it's weird. I have to wonder if it's a telepathic alien cat or a regular ole domestic cat, or if there is even a difference. I spot a black one, dancing on the top of an aged wooden fence, its yellow eyes sweeping over me and I stop and it stops. I stare. It stares. My heart starts thumping in my chest. And then it hisses and scampers off.

Just another cat in this world that hates me. Not the descendent of the cat I am looking for.

As the road slopes towards downtown, I pass through a little commercial island amongst the dense residents. I stop at a café and get a burger and just watch the comings and goings of the Seattleites. The place has exposed brick walls and small round tables, smelling of grilling meat and beer.

I left this town after Mia died, after I dealt with all the

things that needed to be dealt with, and I miss the city. But I also feel lonely, lonelier than I was twenty-five years ago when I took a job at a nineties dot-com boom company and moved up here.

Back then, all the greenery felt invasive and the humidity felt unnatural. Now it feels like home, but only to my body, not to my heart.

Without Mia there is no home for me.

After my meal, I wander out and head back toward downtown on Madison when I see another black cat. This time it is on the sidewalk in front of me, its yellow eyes staring at me.

"Hi, kitty," I say, stopping. Cats have always hated me, but now it's different. Now I know it was the big black cat that I defeated over and over as I traveled through Mia's young life. It basically cursed me, telling other cats about me.

"Come on, then, eh," I hear a male voice say. I look around and there are a few other people on the sidewalk, but no one close enough. And that voice has an English accent, one that sounds kind of cockney to my untrained American ear.

"You are the Denier, ain't ya?" the voice says. "Prophesied long ago by the Great One to return to us and deliver us."

I take a step forward and the cat takes a small step backward. The voice I am hearing is clear, unaffected by the noise on the street. It has to be that cat.

"My name is Ash," I say.

"Right," I hear in my head. "It's you. Right on time. Come on then."

The cat trots down the sidewalk and makes a quick turn up into a residential area.

I follow. And it's not nearly as weird as when Angelica Huston "saved" my life. But let's face it, it's pretty darn weird.

CHAPTER THIRTY-SIX

THE STREET IS steep and I'm breathing heavy as I rush after the telepathic cat. It's a black one, like the one I fought a few decades ago (objective time, not subjective time, mind you), but it's smaller and seems quite young, its black fur sleek and very well groomed. He has a splash of white under his nose, looking very much like a tiny mustache, and a triangle of white on his chest.

Its path is erratic, it jumps on a low wall, and then dashes into some hedges, and then sprints across a street. I am working hard to keep up, thinking, yet again, that time travelers need to be in better shape than I am.

He called me the "Denier" and talked about a prophecy "The Great One" had uttered. About how I will "deliver" them.

"Can you slow down?" I get out between breaths as we head up a steeper hill.

The cat jumps on a low grey boulder fronting an uncharacteristically unkempt yard with weeds invading the overgrown bushes of white and yellow daisies.

"Ya ain't much, are ya?" the cat asks as it licks its paw and starts washing its face.

I lean down, hands on my knees, and just breathe. "It's been a hell of a few days," I say.

"You sure you are this Ash?" he asks in my head. "The denier of dreams and the defender of our enemy." He pauses and sniffs. "Oy. There it is. I smell the burning fluid ya used in your battle with The Great One. It must be you."

I stare at the cat, its unblinking yellow eyes staring right back at me.

"What is your name?" I ask. Not because it's a relevant question or anything, but because my brain is stumbling on this new development. I found the cats, but I'm supposed to save them? The same cats I intend to use?

"It's Charlie Chaplin," he says. "Have you seen that bloke? He's funny, that one. He don't have to say a word and you're laughing your arse off, you are."

Shit. Do all telepathic cats and dogs have British accents and have they all taken on the name of an actor or actress? Are they all obsessed with movies and television?

I feel dizzy, and it's not just from the exercise. I stumble forward and find a rock to sit on next to Charlie Chaplin.

"Do you mind if I call you Charlie?" I ask.

The cat sniffs and backs up a step. "That I do," he says. "My name is Charlie *Chaplin*."

What the hell? Angelical Huston is also obsessed with me addressing her by both her names. I swear this says something important about their societies.

"Are you all right there?" the cat asks.

I shake my head. "No," I say. "I am not all right. I came looking for you, so you can help me steal Angelica Huston's spaceship. There is something I need to do."

I'm looking down, smelling the mild earthy smell of the daisies behind me, feeling sweat trickle down my lower back, so I don't catch the cat's expression, but I feel a change in its demeanor. It moves next to me and starts rubbing its body against my thigh, the rumble of a purr escaping its chest.

Now remember, the big black cat cursed me, made it so all cats everywhere seemed to hate me. I've never really experienced this before, not since I was a kid.

Instinctively my hand goes to the cat and its silky fur slides beneath my hand. I had never understood cat people before, but I think I might now. It's this glorious bit of affection from the often aloof feline that makes the haughty nature of them worth it.

"I knew it!" the cat says in my head, his voice loud. "You are the Denier and the Deliverer. You are the one The Great One spoke of. You are here to save us."

WHAT AM I supposed to do? Say, "I'm sorry, Charlie Chaplin, but I'm only here so I can convince you to be a prop in some theater I need to conduct so I can do what I need to do."

My scratches from battling the big black cat, "The Great One," are still healing and I don't want any more. But that's not why I don't say that. It's the wholehearted affection. It's the fact that the cat needs me. It's the tiny bit of perspective in this alien cats versus alien dogs battle.

I swallow hard and ask a harder question while I pet Charlie Chaplin. "What is it I'm supposed to do for you?"

The cat stops and the rumbling purr quickly dies.

"Eh?" he says in my head. "You don't know?"

"I'm afraid not," I say.

The cat slips from beneath my hand and goes back to the rock. The sun is still beating down and I really should take the duster off, but all my squirt guns are in there and it would be very awkward walking around with my water cannon hanging from my shoulder harness.

"This ain't what I expected," he says.

"Me too," I say.

We're just staring at each other as the sun beats down on us and a car drives by. As bees buzz in the daisies behind us and I continue to sweat.

"Well… there's nothing for it then," the cat says. "Come on along, we'll have to let Bette Davis decide what to do about you."

"What to do…?" I mumble, reaching into my pocket and making sure my ultrasonic gizmo is still there. There is something in his tone that is worrisome.

"Yeah," he says. "With you. What to do with you."

"You mean besides steal a time-traveling spaceship from a telepathic canine?" I ask.

Charlie Chaplin stares at me again, those yellow eyes reminding me of the big black cat I battled, reminding me why I consider myself a dog person. Now that the happy purring is done, the predator is back.

"It's not about the stealin'," he says. "It's what we do with the bloody ship, and if you are the Deliverer why the 'ell don't you know what to do with it?"

"And if I'm not this Deliverer?" I ask.

"Let's just say you want to be the Deliverer," he says. "Now let's get goin'."

Charlie Chaplin slinks away, but I stand there for a moment. I'm scared. I'll admit it. Even with habanero-spiked squirt guns and my ultrasonic gizmo, I'm scared. I have the scratches to prove that such fears are well founded.

But I need the cats to steal the ship, so with my hand in my pocket holding my ultrasonic gizmo, I follow Charlie Chaplin.

CHAPTER THIRTY-SEVEN

THE JAPANESE GARDENS in Washington Park are breathtaking. Particularly in the full sun. Meandering paths, a pond full of koi and blooming lotuses, manicured trees, arched bridges, stone pagodas, blooming flowers.

This, in many ways, is Seattle to me. People tend to be a little quieter and a little more respectful here, the sacred nature of the space palpable.

Mia and I used to come here. Often. Especially after a fight or a misunderstanding. "Gardens," one of us would say and we would get in the car and drive here, walk the paths, smell the flowers, hear the gurgle of water until we were suddenly holding hands and whatever disagreement we had didn't seem so big anymore.

I follow Charlie Chaplin back into Washington Park and as soon as it's clear where we are going, I feel myself calming down.

He climbs a tree and hops over the fence on Lake Washington Boulevard and tells me to meet him inside.

I have a moment. I can get away. I can give up this madness of time travel and domesticated pets that are actually aliens and slink back to my life and try to forget about this, try to get over Mia.

But Mia. I have to fix this. I have to make it right.

I pay for my ticket and go in the human entrance. At first, I don't see any cats. I take a moment and just breathe in the peace and tranquility. Phoenix has the Desert Botanical Gardens, which are spectacular in their own way, full of prickly desert beauty, but to me nothing matches the verdant Zen of Seattle's Japanese Garden.

I forget about aliens as my feet start on the familiar path, as I breathe in the moist floral air, as my eyes linger on the meticulously groomed trees, the cement pagodas covered in moss, and the lush flowers.

I breathe deeply and it feels like Mia is here, like she is walking next to me, but we aren't holding hands yet. I turn my head to the side a little to deepen the illusion. I haven't been here since she died, and I am regretting that.

I thought it would be too much of her here for me to enjoy it. And maybe it would have been right after she died, but now the way I feel her here is just perfect.

For a few minutes, there is no mission, there is only this moment in this garden feeling my beloved. Love and partnership was something I wanted, but I always doubted it was possible for me. But Mia changed all of that.

Mia.

The infinite Möbius strip of my time travel, of my seeking

to see her during her last rally, of her terrible experience. I need to stop it from happening over and over as the past and the future become one with this time-travel madness. I need to stop it. I need to break the Möbius strip.

"You'll figure it out," I almost hear Mia's voice say. She's not speaking to me, but it's almost like she is. "With that sci-fi obsessed, engineering brain of yours, you'll figure it out. I have faith in you."

Mia is not really here. I'm too much of an engineer to believe in ghosts. But the Mia that is in my heart, that is so part of me, is always with me. It is that Mia that is talking to me.

"Thank you, love," I whisper, my feet carrying me along the path, the music of the gurgling water in my ears, the koi in the pond coming close, hoping I have some bread for them to eat.

And the truth is, I had figured it out. Most of it. My plan is to make a time bubble of all of this, all of the time travel I have experienced that revolves around Mia and started with the first disastrous trip to right the wrong of me missing her rally.

My plan is to do away with Ash and return to being Ashton Bach, the lonely sci-fi geek who knows nothing of alien telepathic dogs and the reality of time travel.

But Mia is the problem. In time traveling back with Angelica Huston, I saved her life several times. I had given my younger self the nudge he needed to go meet Mia in that bar in the nineties. There is no Mia without time travel. There is no Mia and me without time travel.

And then I remember Charlie Chaplin. The cats can help. They can comfort the twelve-year-old Mia behind her house when her parents are fighting. They can be there at the high school and delay her crossing the street and being hit by the car. They can provide small little interventions at the exact right moments.

But what about the bar? What about the nudge the young me needs to go say hello to Mia? I remember it. I remember the old disheveled guy in his duster who looked like he was homeless and stank of spicy food. And now I remember being that guy.

But that isn't the important part. That I get a nudge is what is important and it doesn't have to be me giving that nudge. Jessica Cole could do it. Anyone could do it. But how to get them to?

"Hey there, Ash," I hear a voice say in my head. "I don't really think talkin' to yourself is such a great thing. You look the fool. Now come along, Bette Davis will see you."

Startled out of my reverie, I look around. There are a few people here, none of them paying attention to me. Across the grass towards the tall trees that border Lake Washington Boulevard, I see a black cat pacing back and forth nervously.

Well, they want something from me and I want something from them. They can take my place in Mia's life. They can convince Jessica to intervene in the bar. But what is it that the cats want? What am I supposed to deliver them from?

CHAPTER THIRTY-EIGHT

BETTE DAVIS IS a Siamese cat with white fur accented by black points on her face, paws, and the tips of her ears. She also has those slightly crossed freaky blue eyes. She's a big cat and is deep in the cool of the trees when I see her.

She turns slowly, those eyes taking me in, something vaguely accusing about them. She's clearly intelligent and calculating, and formidable. I put my hand into my duster pocket and grip my ultrasonic gizmo. My untested ultrasonic gizmo, I might add.

Some of you reading this may be cat people, you may be wondering at my reaction. Thinking that a big growling dog would be a lot more terrifying. And, depending on the dog, it could be. But in my mind, a growling dog is almost always about territory. Give it space and you'll probably be just fine. A cat, on the other hand, is a much more mysterious creature.

And you have to remember that I've been getting

scratched by cats for no apparent reason my entire adult life. I've never been bitten by a dog.

"Well, well, well," Bette Davis says in my head. "Look what the cat dragged in."

Bette's voice is silky smooth, so smooth that the tired cliché takes a moment to sink it. And the fact that an alien cat said it. She too has an English accent, but a cultured one unlike Charlie Chaplin.

I just stand there, my plan evaporating in my head. I'm not going to convince this cat to do anything it doesn't want to, much less the precise things that need to be done to replace me in Mia's young life.

She just stares at me and I quickly get the impression that if this is a staring contest then I am hopelessly outmatched.

I decide to keep this simple. To forget about what they want of me and just try to get what I need. I pull out my ultrasonic gizmo and gesture with it.

"I'm an engineer," I say, licking my lips. "I've been in Angelica Huston's ship long enough to understand how it works. This will open the hatch."

I press the middle button and an electronic beep is emitted. Not the ultrasonics I wired up, just a silly beep for show.

The Siamese just cocks her head slightly, her blue-eyed gaze steady. I can hear the cars on Lake Washington Boulevard. They are drowning out the calm gurgling of the pond and I miss it.

I put the gizmo back and pull out the gloves I made. I put them on and trigger the LEDS that flash along the fingertips. It's a cheap trick, but I'm hoping it is enough.

"With these, I can fly the ship," I say. I slowly take them

off and put them away. Bette Davis is still staring at me and Charlie Chaplin is too.

"I need your help stealing the ship," I say. "Tomorrow just before eleven at a house not far from here. Help me steal the ship and I'll do what I can for you." I pause, but they are both still staring at me. "Come along and I'll show you the house."

I turn to leave and they are still silent, but I don't hesitate. I take several steps and I hear Bette Davis say in my head, "Charlie Chaplin here tells me that you are our Deliverer and yet you know not what you deliver us from."

I pause but don't turn. "And yet I know you will help me steal the ship."

"And if we don't?" she asks.

I shrug, trying to keep myself calm. Trying to not listen to the yammering voice in my head that tells me I have no clue what I am doing. That I am still Ashton Bach, grieving geek, not Ash the time traveler.

I let it go and say what I think Ash would say. "This has happened before, that is how I know it will happen again. Follow me now if you want to be part of it. If you don't, I'm sure I'll find some other cats. The ship will be stolen, the question is whether you'll be there or not."

IS THIS HOW A BADASS FEELS? Terrified most of the time?

Jessica Cole, she's clearly a badass. From head to foot for all her life, I suspect. Does she feel such doubt when she's being all decisive and brave?

My legs are rubber as I walk down the paths of the Japanese Garden, barely hearing the gurgle of the pond or noticing the mottled orange flash of the koi.

I like Charlie Chaplin, and when he was purring and affectionate, I wanted to do nothing more than to help him. But Bette Davis just creeps me out. And maybe the cats do need help, but that is not for me to do. I just want to be Ash long enough to get Ashton Bach his quiet little life back.

I think I hear the quiet padding of feet behind me, but I am not sure. I walk steadily out of the park and head towards the house. It takes everything I've got, but I don't look back.

If they don't follow, I'll have to find some other cats. Maybe I can go to the shelter and get a few cats from there to go along with the theater of stealing the ship. Maybe there are other telepathic alien cats around here.

I mean, what I said about this happening before and that it will happen again, is true. It has. It will. I just don't know how the dots connect.

"You know, I must say," I hear a male voice with a cockney accent say in my head. "Now that was impressive. Treatin' the mighty Bette Davis like that. Man, you are a fierce ape if ever there was one. You must be the Deliverer. I called it. Charlie Chaplin knows his legends, that he does."

I may not feel like a badass, but it seems like I look like one to a telepathic alien cat who calls himself Charlie Chaplin.

I smile and keep walking.

CHAPTER THIRTY-NINE

I CAN'T SLEEP. I know I need to. If my first round with Angelica Huston taught me anything it's that a time traveler should be well rested before they start time traveling, because once you get on that roller coaster, you never know when you are going to have a break.

And I have a break and I can't sleep.

After showing Charlie Chaplin the house, after hearing more of his awed praises and self-congratulatory pratter about finding me, I walked down Madison towards downtown and found a hotel.

Charlie followed me, but kept his distance. I let him. A badass wouldn't care, although I did find it a little creepy.

The buildings in this part of town get taller the closer to downtown you get, most of them taller than the trees. I'm on the top floor of a five-story hotel with views of taller glass buildings and the bustling Broadway Avenue.

I'm fed. I'm hydrated. I'm showered. I'm exhausted. And

I'm awake, pacing over the short grey carpet in my bare feet, wrapped in the comforting terry-cloth robe of the hotel, my long, wet hair hanging down past my shoulders, not constrained by a ponytail for once.

Earlier, when I convinced Angelica Huston I knew what I was doing, I had a plan. It was simple enough.

One. Find some cats and steal the ship.

Two. Execute the maneuver that pushed Angelica and I into the alternate timeline where humanity hadn't evolved on Earth.

Three. Go back to Phoenix right before Angelica Huston went to save me from the truck crashing through my apartment wall and stop her.

This would, I believed, make a time bubble of all the madness. It would leave a version of me in my apartment, programming away to the tunes of Journey on a Saturday. There would be no truck crashing through my apartment because she wouldn't leave an exhausted me to do it after jaunting through time with her. It would restore Ashton Bach to his rightful place in the world, an Ashton Bach that never went back in time to see his dead wife and hopefully moves on with his life.

As I pace. As I review works of time-travel fiction, I struggle to see the tangle of it clearly. The past can't be changed, but it can be changed. There will be a time-bubble version of this sealed off, surrounded by the altered timeline, healed over like a wound, and the timeline goes on as if it never happened.

Angelica Huston already did this once with that disastrous visit with Mia, and I had thought I could do it again with me. With all of this.

But I failed to realize something essential about time bubbles. You can't seal yourself in one, someone else has to. Like Angelica Huston did with her first time jump with me.

And then I go over in my head how Angelica Huston created the time bubble. She didn't tell me exactly, but I work it out the best I can.

One. She jumps to Phoenix, convinces me to go with her —she's a telepathic dog, not much to convince me of—and we go back in time to Mia's rally, Mia recognizes that I shouldn't be there and freaks out, and I lose it afterward. Angelica returns the traumatized me back to my time.

Two. She jumps back to Phoenix, but a little earlier. She "saves" me from the truck smashing into my apartment and we skip through time interacting with the young Mia. This, I believe, she had intended to do after our initial visit that turned out so poorly.

The second jump, the one earlier in time, seals that mistake away. It can't happen again, because she jumped back earlier and inserted herself into the timeline in a different way. For once it wasn't a Möbius strip of causality. This was the "first" time that it had happened. (I put "first" in quotes because this is time travel, such terms are hardly unambiguous.)

So that was how she created a time bubble.

As I am coming to understand the rules of time travel, the timeline resists forking. A small thing like this, it will heal over, thus the bubble. A major change and the timeline forks and you have an alternate reality. Apparently, the latter is frowned upon by Angelica's canine superiors.

So given that understanding, it is now clear that I can't time bubble all of this myself.

And then it hits me and my knees get weak and I stumble to the king bed and sit down.

"The cats," I mumble. "The cats can seal me in."

I thought I had understood the "evil" me. The one that stole the spaceship. I thought I had already become Ash the time traveler.

I was wrong.

Ash the time traveler is the one that is willing to give control of the most powerful technology the universe has ever seen to the alien felines just so he can seal himself away in a time bubble.

But my ultrasonic gizmo is a fake, except for the ultrasonic part, and my LED flashy gloves are definitely a fake. I will have possession of a time-traveling spaceship, but I don't actually know how to use it, so how can I give control of it to the felines so they can bubble me in?

Am I actually considering this?

Only a few hours ago I couldn't conceive of really being evil Ash, now it seems like the only way out.

I start pacing again. I don't think I'm going to be able to sleep tonight.

CHAPTER FORTY

THE FATEFUL DAY of stealing Angelica Huston's time-traveling spaceship dawns and I sleep right through it. I set an alarm on my phone earlier, while I was still pacing, and its blaring insistence slowly penetrates through my sodden consciousness.

I am dreaming, some crazy swashbuckling pirate dream where I'm surrounded by cats standing on their rear legs and wielding sabers. The biggest one is a Siamese with piercing blue eyes. "Walk the plank, ya will," she says.

"Walk the plank!" a parrot echoes from the cat's shoulder. "Down to Davey Jones's Locker."

The buzzing saves me and I wake with a start, my cheek nearly glued to the mauve bedspread by my dried drool. At some point when the morning was getting close, I flopped on the bed and finally slept.

I must tell you that I am a man of a certain age and such

flopping and such careless sleep comes at a heavy price. My neck has a painful crick in it and my eyes are nearly glued shut.

I moan. A lot. Most definitely not a badass right now. Just a middle-aged man who didn't take proper care of his aging body.

I moan some more and crawl to the phone. 9 AM. I have some time. I turn off the alarm and stumble into the shower and let the hot water beat on me. It doesn't actually return me to a fully human state, but I become more functional.

I stumble through getting ready, making sure my squirt guns are full, my ultrasonic gizmo is in good shape, and getting dressed. I stumble down to the hotel restaurant for a few bites of eggs with my coffee. It's one of those breakfast buffets hotels have setup these days to lure folks away from the vacation rentals. The tables are tall and you have to sit on a stool, but I get a spot where I can see the traffic on Broadway. The sky is steel grey, and the light is diffuse and it feels way more like Seattle to me.

My head hurts, just like I have a hangover, even though I had nothing to drink last night. Thank you very much, middle age.

I try to get my mind in gear, but there is only one way out of this. I have to give the cats the spaceship. I have to hope they can figure out how to use it. I have to be Evil Ash.

And yes. Evil is capitalized above because if I do this, it seems like that word deserves a capital letter. The time-travel technology belongs to the canines. Angelica Huston has made very clear that it is the most powerful technology the universe has ever seen. And if I turn that technology over to her enemies just to try to contain my personal suffering then I am truly Evil with a capital "E."

But I can't do that.

I can't.

I am not Evil with a capital "E." I am just Ashton with a capital "A."

Even if the cats could figure out how to operate the ship, I can't give it to them. I have to do the bit of theater and get the ship back to Angelica Huston. Just another stupid bit of Möbius strip casualty in this crazy time-travel business.

I sigh and stare into my coffee, hoping the caffeine will finally kick in.

"It's going to be okay, kid."

I freeze. I don't look up right away. The voice is familiar, and as I wind it back in my head, I did hear a chair scraping across from me while I tried to desperately figure this thing out.

The voice is male and a little rough, but oddly familiar. I can't quite place it. An old friend from Seattle, maybe? Have I been discovered? Will I have to create some awkward lie about why I am here? Why I am dressed this way.

"What's going to be okay?" I quietly ask, still not looking.

"Life," he says. "The universe. And everything."

He just dropped the title of the third Hitchhiker's Guide to the Galaxy book. My heart does its best to thump rapidly in my chest, but it seems to be too tired to put on too good of a show.

It can't be.

I slowly look up at the old man sitting across from me. He's tall and lanky with short steel-grey hair buzzed down to about half an inch. His face is deeply wrinkled like he's spent plenty of time in the sun and his brown eyes are thin slits below his bushy grey eyebrows.

There is a scar on his face. Not Bond villain level, but very noticeable. It runs from the right side of his nose about an inch diagonally, making a very strange frown line.

I'm looking at Ash the time traveler. An older version of myself. He looks to be in his seventies and he really does look like a badass.

He actually looks somewhat muscular in a form-fitting black sweater and there is something about the set of his jaw and the quirk of his smile.

"Do you... I mean... Is this..." I stammer, the words not quite forming properly. It doesn't seem like my older self should be seeking me out.

"Listen, kid," he says. And I don't like being called "kid," but he does appear to be old enough to be my father. "I'm not staying. I just want to say my piece and I'll leave you to it."

I swallow hard and nod, not daring to speak.

"You're wondering if there is a way to bubble all of this," he begins, licking his lips and nodding vaguely towards the street. "One that doesn't involve giving the ship to the cats. There is. You'll figure it out. But let me say that if you do that, you'll miss out on a lot. It's been a hell of a ride."

Looking at him, I can believe that. The wrinkles lining his face speak of years, maybe difficult years. But there is something else. An energy and an ease that I do not possess.

"But Mia," I say quietly.

"That mistake has already been bubbled," he says with a shrug, but I notice his eyes darkening and flicking away. "What do you gain by sealing it all away?"

"My life," I say. "I get my simple, quiet life back."

He just stares at me and I feel compelled to continue.

"Mia was my—our—everything. And this... it has... it has ripped it back open. I can't see her during her rally, undo my mistake, and I can't stop feeling guilty about it. I miss her all over again." I stop and sigh. "I... I think that I'm too old for this," I say.

He smiles, his eyes twinkling, and then he laughs. It's the kind of full-bodied unrestrained laughter that I have rarely experienced.

"Kid," he begins when he's done laughing. "I won't tell you that age is just a number, because I feel the years, believe me I feel them. And I won't tell you there is any easy way through your grief, because there isn't. But just because life has knocked you down and you lost something precious and just because your body is slowing down a touch doesn't mean that it's time to stop living."

I nod and remember another reason. "The plastic smell," I say. "Feeling like I'm breaking out with the hives. The nausea that occurs during the jumps. Something is happening in my limbic lobe."

He nods and rubs at his short hair. I glimpse a long scar on top of his head. "Yeah. That," he says. "You already know I can't tell you much about it, but let me say this." He leans close, his eyes so intense as they stare into mine. "You bubble all of this and you'll never find out what that means.

"I've had a good life, kid, and your time bubble can't take that away from me. But I hate to see you miss out on it."

I open my mouth to speak, but he is up and walking away. I watch him stride confidently out the door and into the grey Seattle morning.

CHAPTER FORTY-ONE

SO, we have a time-traveling spaceship that I need to steal with the assistance of telepathic cats. We have Jessica Cole and a relationship that may or may not be real despite my attempt to create a Möbius strip of causality out of it. Then there is the felines and me being their Denier and the Deliverer, whatever the hell that is. And now my decades future-self stopped by and hinted at an intriguing and adventurous future.

I haven't had enough sleep for this, and I don't even know if there is enough sleep for this.

Sitting in the hotel, staring at the door my decades future-self walked out of, my brain finally engages and I realize there is a lot more he can tell me, but by the time I get out on the street, he is gone.

"Oy. Ya do look like what the cat drug in this morning, you do." Charlie Chaplin is sitting on top of an old beat-up newspaper stand. I look around, not for other cats, but out of concern for this one. This is not the kind of neighborhood for a cat. We aren't fully in the business district of downtown, but this is no longer a quiet neighborhood.

"Come on," I say, holding out my hands. The cat jumps into my palms and quickly climbs to my shoulder.

"Look, all ya sods," he says. "Look here. Charlie Chaplin has his very own ape, he does."

I groan and start walking back up Madison. I haven't had enough sleep or enough coffee for this. The day is clouding up and much more Seattle-like, so there is that, at least.

"Onward, ape!" Charlie shouts in my mind, his claws digging into my duster as I lengthen my stride heading us towards the yard that Angelica Huston will be landing her time-traveling spaceship in shortly.

I still don't have a plan, not a real one, but time does not care for my lack of a plan. It is time to steal the most powerful technology in the universe.

OKAY, so a time bubble is possible for me and all of this madness without giving the ship to the cats. My future-self made that clear. But how?

Maybe I go back to Phoenix, to right before Angelica Huston found me the second time when she was time bubbling that me in from that disastrous trip to see Mia during her rally. And then I—

"Why so quiet, there, ape?" Charlie Chaplin asks from my shoulder.

The retail area is gone and a four-story apartment looms

close to the road, the occasional tree making it feel less city-like. Madison is still two lanes in each direction, but it's late in the morning so traffic is not bad.

"I'm thinking," I say.

"I'm a good thinker," he says in my head. "Clearly I am. I located you real quick, didn't I? So lay it on me, Deliverer. What can Charlie Chaplin help you think about today?"

"Nothing," I say, taking a deep breath. The air smells of exhaust, but behind that is the damp, vaguely floral scent that is Seattle. "I just need to think."

"Charlie Chaplin knows a thing or two, he does," he says.

We walk past a bank and then a Chinese food place, the rich smells wafting out and reminding me that I hardly got a bite of food in this morning.

"Do you know what a Möbius strip is?" I ask, hoping to deter him and get him quiet so I can think.

"Well of course I do," he says. "August Möbius was a good bloke and loved to have cats around. Found their calm demeanor and meticulous grooming habits laudable. You apes don't remember it this way, but it was a cat that invented the Möbius strip, it was."

"What?" I ask, stopping, the scent of fried meat still hanging thick in the air.

"I am telling ya the God's honest truth," he says with sincerity, and I have to wonder what notion cats have of God. I mean, didn't the ancient Egyptians worship cats? And what do I think of that being in the "I have no freaking clue" camp when it comes to God and an afterlife.

"How did a cat invent the Möbius strip?" I ask.

"We felines, we be a smart lot, you see?" he says. "Such

simple geometric concepts ain't beyond us. One of my ancestors saw the poor bloke struggling with the idea so she just happened to twist a piece o' paper just the right way so the fine August Möbius could see it."

I just stand there staring down the street, my mind having slipped into neutral.

"Space travelers we were," Charlie Chaplin continues, his tone hushed. "Rulers we were on a planet orbiting the star you call Vega in the Lyra constellation. Educated we were when we came here. Of course, we had mastered geometry as simple as what August Möbius was foolin' around with."

My brain starts up and some things come into focus. When Angelica Huston called the pack, I saw the big canine spaceship, the one used for abducting and studying humans. That spaceship is full of dogs and it would be hard to take over. Angelica Huston's spaceship is just her and definitely the one you would target if you wanted to steal a canine spaceship.

Maybe they don't care about the most powerful technology in the universe. Maybe they just want to go home.

"Charlie Chaplin," I begin as I start slowly walking towards the house. "Are you and Bette Davis just trying to get home?"

"I knew you were the Deliverer!" the cat shouts in my head as its claws dig into my shoulder. "I knew it, I did. Yes indeed, we are tryin' to get home."

I speed my pace up, suddenly more awake and feeling a little hopeful. Off the top of my head, I didn't know how far away Vega was, but I knew it was a relatively close star to the Earth. Maybe something could actually be done for the cats.

Maybe I could figure out how to complete my own time bubble with their help.

"And go back in time, of course," he continues. "And right the wrongs that happened to our lineage there thousands of years ago. We were banished to the Earth, we were. But the Deliverer will take us home and take us back in time!"

So much for any of this being simple. I groan and keep walking.

CHAPTER FORTY-TWO

ALIEN TELEPATHIC FELINES HAVE EGOS. It's quite clear by Charlie Chaplin's behavior and the story he tells me of feline royalty on a planet in the Vega system and a coup that sent them on a one-way trip to a backwater planet called Earth.

The canines have egos too, I am sure, but for the purpose of this moment, it's the feline ego that is important.

Egos are tricky things. Our sense of self and identity are crucial to our survival in the rough world of biology, but those egos are so good at fooling themselves.

Charlie Chaplin told me a cat-oriented story of the origin of the Möbius strip. Was there a cat there playing with a piece of paper? Sure, I buy that. Did that cat inspire August Möbius? Yeah, that makes sense too. Was the cat doing it on purpose to help August Möbius? I don't know, but I guess it wasn't surprising that an intelligent telepathic cat had a cat-centric view of the world.

"It was the Egyptians, it was, that took us in right and proper," Charlie Chaplin says. The apartments have fallen behind as I walk us up Madison into the fully residential area. "Made our exile not so terrible. They worshiped Bast, a goddess created in our image, they did."

I am not going to say, with my limited experience, that all cats have a bigger ego than all dogs. I will say that Charlie Chaplin had a much bigger ego than Angelica Huston, at least as measured by how they expressed themselves.

The grade is starting to make me sweat under my dark duster and that is helpful. It is clearing out the cobwebs and my brain is starting to work. It is clear to me that if I need to manipulate the cats to get them to help me, it will be easy because of that ego of theirs.

It is not lost on me that the theme of their mission—righting a perceived wrong—is exactly the same as mine when I set out to find Angelica Huston and right the wrong of me missing Mia's rally.

But sometimes it's better to leave the past in the past.

As we near the house, which is east of Madison Street and south of Washington Park, the cats begin to gather.

First, it's a tabby shadowing us as we head up Madison. Then it's a big black cat, and by the time we turn off Madison we have an entourage. Some on the sidewalk behind us, some capering across the yards parallel to us, some peeking out from behind trees up ahead. It's like some crazy cat food commercial where I have the food they all crave and it's meow-elicious or some such foolishness like that.

Charlie Chaplin greets each new cat, saying something

like, "He's the Deliverer, he is, a good ape if ever there was one. Join Charlie Chaplin and let's take our world back."

I didn't need to fool the cats at all. Just listening to Charlie Chaplin and being a tiny bit perceptive was plenty. It makes me wonder what they have been through to be so desperate.

They were royalty in the Vega system. They were banished to Earth, which wasn't so bad at first because of how the ancient Egyptians treated them. In our modern era they are no longer royalty, no longer gods (but clearly pampered). When you think about it, this explains a hell of a lot about cats.

The neighborhood is quiet, the sounds of children playing and the occasional car the only noises. There are sidewalks on both sides of the street with well-tended grass, a variety of trees from tall pines to shorter fruit trees, to big maples. The neighborhood is old but in good shape and again reminds me of where Mia and I used to live.

As we approach the street the house is on, Bette Davis is sitting atop a cement wall staring at me with her freaky blue eyes, the wall tall enough so that we are eye to eye.

"That is far enough," she says, her gaze intense, her eyes slightly crossed as she stares at me.

I had gotten so comfortable with Charlie Chaplin that I had forgotten about all my preparations. I stop and reach my hand into my duster and grab ahold of my ultrasonic gizmo.

"Good morning, Bette Davis," I say cheerfully. "How are you today?"

She leans forward and sniffs at me, her little black nose almost wrinkling like she smelled something awful. I am still armed with habanero-spiked squirt guns.

"He's the Deliverer, he is," Charlie Chaplin says, but his tone is less exuberant in front of Bette Davis.

"Are you?" Bette Davis asks.

I shrug, feeling the weight of Charlie Chaplin on my shoulder. "I am going to steal a time-traveling spaceship. Right now. Do you want to come along?"

"Such an ape," the cat says in my head. "Not answering a direct question directly. So simple and still you can't do it."

"Deliverer is your term, not mine," I say with a smile. "Only you can judge if that is what I am."

I feel the cats draw close, there must be at least twenty of them. I switch my grip on the ultrasonic gizmo so my thumb is above the button that triggers all the ultrasonic bark deterrent devices I cobbled together. It's still in the pocket of my duster but will work just fine there.

"Are you the Deliverer?" she asks, her tone too calm. This is clearly a test and I suspect there will be plenty of pain forthcoming if I fail. I feel Charlie Chaplin stiffen on my shoulder and the cats move a little closer.

"I can't be this Deliverer if we don't get moving," I say, nodding in the direction of the house. I don't know why, but I just can't lie to them outright. I'm happy to let them draw their own conclusions, but I don't want to go so far as to tell them I can make all their dreams come true.

Because I can't.

I've got a preprogrammed spaceship and some theatrical aids and that is it.

"Are you the Deliverer?" Bette Davis asks again.

Okay, so I understand that the crossed-eyed thing with Siamese cats is a genetic defect, putting their retinas a little off center so their eyes look crossed when they are looking straight at something... or someone. Like me. I get the reason, but it still kind of freaks me out.

I take a deep breath and try to calm myself, the cats inching closer, a few of them starting to hiss. I somehow doubt that my ultrasonic gizmo will drive them all off, and I only have two hands to hold squirt guns and that won't be effective here.

"If you are asking if I can take you back in time, back to Vega so you can reclaim what is yours..." I trail off. All the cats are quiet and Bette Davis's jaw is hanging open, her fangs showing, as if she is getting ready to eat something.

"So... so you can reclaim your planet," I continue. "I will do everything I can to make that happen."

"He's the Deliverer, he is," Charlie Chaplin crows from my shoulder. "I told ya. I told ya!"

Bette Davis continues to hold my gaze but then her head lowers and she begins to purr. I find myself petting her without even thinking about it.

What have I done?

CHAPTER FORTY-THREE

HERE'S THE THING. I made a promise to the cats, but I apparently did it just like an ape. I said, "I will do everything I can to make that happen."

I said it knowing I do not have the means to take them to Vega when they want to go. But I am the man my parents raised and I believe in keeping my word.

But I don't know a thing about what happened on Vega thousands of years ago or the impact changing that would have—provided I could figure out a way to do that.

I've read enough, seen enough movies to know that messing with the timeline often makes things worse. A lot worse.

The cat entourage is swirling around me as I walk to the house like I am some Pied Piper for cats. Like I am some kind of savior. Some of the younger ones are cavorting—there is no other word for it. They are leaping and rolling and climbing up trees and jumping down from trees.

A woman walks out of her house, her terrier on a leash, and her eyes go wide and the dog whines and pulls the woman back into the house.

I am a dog person not a cat person.

But not today.

We walk to the white house with the unique windows and all the cement in the terraced front yard. We walk around to the backyard with all the towering pine trees and the silver bone-shaped spaceship is there, a corgi having just hopped out, the ship irises closed behind her.

Angelica Huston.

From the past... or rather, my past.

"Anyone hurts the corgi and the deal is off," I say, my voice coming out as a hissing snarl. As if being around all these cats has changed me.

I stop, the cats stop, and Angelica freezes and our eyes meet. Her deep soulful brown eyes, the eyes that seem to be able to see right into my soul, look right at me.

I see a moment of shock, and then recognition, and then sorrow so deep I just want to weep. I am about to betray her and she knows it. In this moment, I am most definitely Evil Ash the time traveler.

"You heard the Deliverer," Bette Davis says in my head, her voice loud but distant like she is projecting it to all the cats. "No hurting the dog. But scare her good."

Except for Charlie Chaplin on my shoulder and Bette Davis at my side, the cats tear off hissing and yowling.

Angelica Huston stares at me for one more moment and I feel my heart breaking. There is nothing better than the trust of a dog, and there is nothing worse than losing that trust.

Well. Okay, that last bit is slightly hyperbolic. I mean, losing Mia was way worse, but that is the way it feels in the moment.

And then Angelica Huston lets out a frightened yip, turns tail, and runs.

I am truly Evil Ash the time traveler and I don't like the way it feels. Not one bit.

PART FOUR

THE TIME BUBBLE THING

CHAPTER FORTY-FOUR

WHAT WOULD Evil Ash the time traveler do?

That's the question that runs through my head as the cats chase a yelping Angelica Huston off. That sound of the corgi squealing in fright breaks my heart, but I don't have time for a broken heart. I don't have time to feel too much.

I have to figure out how to seal myself into a time bubble. Now more than ever I am convinced of it. Despite the visit from my future-self and his completely vague references to a life worth living. Why couldn't he do better than that? Give me a real reason. No, Evil Ash needs to be just a blip in the radar, just a bubble in the timeline, but it's going to take Evil Ash to figure out how to do it.

I shake off the weight of the promise I made to the cats. If this is all sealed away in a time bubble, such things don't matter. Right now, I need the ship and I need to get rid of the cats.

"Now it is time for you to deliver, Deliverer," Bette Davis says in my head, her voice thick with desire.

"Sorry," I say, pulling out my ultrasonic gizmo and one of my habanero-spiked squirt guns. "I'd really like to help you out, but this particular reality is doomed."

I stride confidently over to the spaceship and turn before the glassy smooth silver side of it where it just closed behind Angelica Huston.

"What?" Bette Davis asks, as she slowly stalks towards me. I feel Charlie Chaplin stiffen on my shoulder, his claws digging into my duster hard enough for me to feel it.

Crap. I should have gotten him off before I started acting so cool. I had just gotten so used to the little cat being there.

I am Evil Ash now, so I do what any villain would do. I take the time to explain my plan to my opponent.

"All of this will soon be in a time bubble," I say. "I am going to stop—" My brain stalls. I want to say "Angelica Huston," but the look she gave me still lingers. I start over. "I am going to stop the *corgi* from ever finding me. I am going back to my old life and so are you. None of this will ever have happened."

I still don't know how to do it. I'm just talking like I do, hoping my brain will solve the puzzle.

Bette Davis is looking towards where the cats ran off, her face focused and the yipping stops and then her freaky blue eyes focus on me. "I don't think so," she says calmly. "I think you are going to take us back home and back in time."

I laugh. It's a brief bark and not at all villain-like. A distant part of me is very disappointed by that. Shouldn't I be managing a mwahahaha or two? "That will never happen,

Bette Davis. The ship is preprogrammed. I worked this out with a future version of... the corgi. This was all a little bit of theatre for your advantage."

There I go again, like some dumb Bond villain explaining everything and wasting time.

"What is that ya say?" Charlie Chaplin asks quietly in my head. "Ya fooled old Charlie Chaplin, ya did? Why, you are a nasty little ape, ain't ya?"

That one hurts too. I am a bit surprised, but the trust of a cat, even a very egotistical one, is a tough thing to lose.

The little black cat jumps down from my shoulder and walks away from me, his tail held high.

I open my mouth to apologize. I am sorry. I hate doing all of this. I want to tell them that if things were different, I would want to find a way. But they aren't and that is Ashton Bach and this is not his show anymore.

I clamp my mouth shut and tighten my grip on my ultrasonic gizmo and my habanero-spiked squirt gun. "Now, please leave before I have to hurt you."

But I was too late. I did too much villain blabbing. The pack of cats are tearing back into the yard, all twenty of them, and they are out for blood. My blood.

CHAPTER FORTY-FIVE

WHEN I SAW MY FUTURE-SELF, the rougher, older, scarred version of me, I thought all of that was a long ways off. That it would take years of time-travel adventure to make me that kind of self-assured badass.

But today, I am really Evil Ash. Betraying both dogs and cats and, annoyingly, doing stupid villain things like blabbing my mouth off about what I am doing and why, and giving all those cats enough time to get back.

And they are mad. Hell hath no fury like a pack of cats scorned.

"He is no Deliverer," Bette Davis says in my head. It has that loud but distant feel and I know she is speaking to all of us. "He is the Deceiver. He is the worst of ape kind and we must end him. Now!"

There are about twenty cats each with eighteen claws and a mouth full of sharp teeth. It's easy to believe they both intend to kill me and can as the mass of them surround me hissing, their backs arched, their tails swatting back and forth, their fangs bared.

This isn't like before with the big black cat and his three or four companions. This isn't them trying to get me out of the way so they can get to the ship. This is them trying to extract revenge on the Deceiver.

As my heart thumps in my chest, I try to keep calm, keep being Evil Ash and figure out what he would do.

I haven't triggered the ultrasonic gizmo. I haven't fired my squirt gun that I have a white-knuckled grip on, the piquant bouquet sharp enough for even my ape nose to smell now that the squirt gun is out. I fear that if I start the fight, they will end it.

"Any last words, Deceiver?" Bette Davis asks, her tail switching restlessly.

I shrug and I try to do it casually. "Just a little note to myself. When deceiving those that trusted you, don't take the time to tell them why and what you are doing."

I back up a step, the cool hard surface of the bone-shaped spaceship pressing into my back. I can make the hatch open, all it takes is a series of knocks, but I don't want half the cats in there with me.

The pack of cats... no, "pack" is what you would use with dogs. The litter of cats... no, that's no good either. That would be a bunch of adorable kittens. What in the world do you call a group of angry cats? Words matter, folks, and not being a cat person I don't know what the right noun is for a collection of angry cats.

I know for crows the noun is "murder," as in the murder of crows rooted through my trash with lethal efficiency.

Stupid name for a bunch of crows, and since I don't know what the right word is for cats, and since it seems to fit, that is the term I am going to use.

Okay, so the *murder* of cats is arrayed in a semicircle around me, all bared fangs and twitching tails. They fear me, or the scratching and biting would have started already. And this isn't like the last time I faced the cats. There will be no Angelica Huston to help me out.

"I'll give you one more chance," I say, waving my ultrasonic gizmo at them. I am happy to report I stop short of blabbing what the device does and losing the element of surprise. But perhaps that is de rigueur for a villain. You blab your little mouth off when you think you have the upper hand and you shut up when the tables inevitably turn.

"One more chance to what?" Bette Davis asks. She is front and center, clearly the leader. I do notice that Charlie Chaplin is not in the ring of cats surrounding me. He is back a few feet, his tale up, his butt pointed right at me.

And I deserve that, I do. I deserve all the disdain the little cat can heap on me. But I don't think I deserve to be murdered by this murder of cats.

See there. "Murder" works pretty well, at least in this situation.

"You have one more chance to leave whole and healthy," I say.

Bette Davis lets out a rhythmic hiss with her fangs fully bared that I have to assume is a laugh. Her head turns to the left and the right and I swear she is talking to all of them and leaving me out of the conversation—unlike a good villain, I might add.

She then slowly turns to me, those freaky blue eyes connecting with mine, and I truly fear for my life. It is the look of a predator that has cornered its prey and is assured of victory.

I don't wait. I press the full-blast button on my ultrasonic gizmo. I fire my habanero-spiked squirt gun at Bette Davis. I knock on cold metal behind me with the end of the ultrasonic gizmo to open the ship. I press my back hard against the cool metal.

I discover something important that Evil Ash shares with Ashton Bach, and maybe this is true for villains in general. We are all afraid to die.

I know, I know, totally obvious. But being a mild-mannered geek and looking out at the badasses of the world, you figure they have a better time with the basic human difficulties than you do. I mean, they are badasses. And I'm not saying I am a full-on badass at this point, but I did just betray Angelica Huston and a murder of desperate cats. Not to mention that I am trying to execute a plan where the ends clearly justify the means.

So I am at the apex of my journey in life so far on the badass meter and I am scared. Terrified. And I so don't want to die.

I am so scared, in fact, that I pee a little bit.

And yes, I am going to fully blame that on terror, not on my middle-aged body and how my bladder has become more fussy the last few years.

So... ultrasonic gizmo activated. Habanero-spiked squirt gun squirting. Cats surging towards me. And I, Evil Ash, at the apex of my badassness, piss myself just a little bit.

CHAPTER FORTY-SIX

MAYBE I'M NOT REALLY a villain. And while on my personal scale I was "Evil" and at an apex of my admittedly low-wattage intentional evil doing, I wasn't that evil. Perhaps not evil enough to be considered a villain.

I am sure I have participated in an array of evils as an over-privileged, consumption-crazed American. And as a bit slinger for hire, I am sure I enabled some terribly amoral corporations to plunder in entirely legal ways.

It is intentional acts of evil that make you a villain. Like betraying Angelica Huston. And yes, a future version of her asked me to do it, but I didn't tell her my plan, my evil plan, was to bubble all of this craziness in for completely selfish reasons.

And the cats, I intentionally misled them and used them.

Totally selfish acts are evil. Betraying others is evil. But does that make me a villain?

Maybe villains only blab like that in the movies. Maybe

my blabbing like that marked me as a decent person doing unusually bad things and that's why it all spilled out like some dumb Bond villain.

And yes, this is what my crazy mind does as twenty snarling, hissing cats launch themselves at me. As time slows down, as claws are fully exposed and fangs are dripping with saliva hungry for my blood, a part of my mind ponders the finer points of evil versus villain.

I did mention that I am a huge sci-fi geek and I have been mainlining that kind of fiction since I was old enough to read, right?

Sci-fi changed me. A lot. Growing up in rather conservative Phoenix reading books by Heinlein and Asimov and Le Guin blew my mind open. Made me see that there were wider possibilities in this world than my rather traditional American upbringing presented to me.

It made the world much bigger and the possibilities seem exciting and pretty much endless.

And while meeting Angelica Huston and time traveling with her has been completely wild and totally beyond anything I imagined, my constant reading made most anything seem possible. I think it helped me adjust to all of this madness as well as I have.

Don't laugh. I think I have adjusted to this most radical of changes fairly well.

So that's one thread of my consciousness, but most of my awareness is on the battle. The ultrasonic gizmo is having an effect. Several cats turn tail and run. Several abort their leaps at me, shaking their heads and yowling in pain.

My habanero-spiked squirt gun is effective, I hit Bette

Davis right in those blue eyes of hers and she holds her ground but doesn't move forward, desperately pawing at her face.

And, yes, I feel bad about that. She's obviously well tended and probably has a cushy home with a loving family that only suspects their cat is an alien—doesn't everyone?—but has no idea she is the local "Great One" and telepathic and plotting to take back her home planet from a rival faction of alien telepathic cats.

During all of this, I am tapping on the hull of the spaceship with my ultrasonic gizmo. It's two sequences I have to deliver. The first one is rather long, and I finish it and stop. I need both hands. Four cats are on me, flying through the air. Maybe they don't have as good of hearing as the others. Maybe they are complete badasses and just don't care.

I get some habanero spray on two of them, but they are flying through the air, it's not like it matters. They all slam into me like some kind of furry cannonballs. One hits my legs. One plows into my groin, and two smash into my chest.

The air is knocked out of me, I am slammed back against the hull of the spaceship, and I almost drop the ultrasonic gizmo, the high-frequency sounds the only thing keeping all of the cats from being on me.

The ship is right behind me so I don't go down. Three of the cats bounce off me, but one is hanging from my groin, its claws digging in.

Yeah, that will wake you up. I have jeans on, so that is some protection, but I feel sharp claws just starting to dig into very tender areas.

Our eyes meet. It's a classic tabby, adorable really, except for those claws and its open mouth as it rears back to bite into my jeans.

I do the only thing I can. First, I scream. Like a girl. Adding an audible screech to the one my gizmo is putting out. And then I shove the squirt gun into its mouth and squeeze and push.

The cat lets go, falling to the ground and landing on its back. Habanero water squirting right down your throat will do that. I feel bad for the cat who is stumbling away, coughing and making the most horrible gacking sound.

Actually we are making a racket. What with the cat yowls and my girlish screams. I hear dogs barking in the neighborhood and a door slamming a house or two away.

I can just imagine what I would say to the cops. "A spaceship? What spaceship? This is just a sculpture I've been working on. The classic dog bone shape is something that has always fascinated me as an artist. And why yes, those are fresh claw marks in the groin of my jeans, but I have no idea how they got there. And the smell? Just the diluted habanero hot sauce I have loaded into the squirt guns I have hiding under this very cool duster."

Because we all know the cats would be long gone by the time the cops got to me. And cats don't get arrested by the police.

There is a moment when I think we all realize it. Bette Davis looks at me with her now bloodshot blue eyes and the rest of the cats freeze. Well, the ones that are still not coughing up habanero water.

"My kind will hunt you for the rest of your life," she hisses in my head. Her ears are back and I can tell the ultrasonic gizmo is making it hard for her to stay here.

Great. Instead of cats always scratching me because of the big black cat that "cursed" me back in 1996, now they'll all be after blood.

Yet another reason to time bubble this in.

Cats start slinking away until it's just Bette Davis facing me with her bloodshot eyes and Charlie Chaplin still facing away, his tail high.

I take my thumb off the button of the ultrasonic gizmo and the relief Bette Davis shows is palpable. Her ears come straight up and she backs up a few steps and paws at her eyes again.

"I really am sorry," I say. "But I am going to put this all in a time bubble, so none of this really matters."

Bette Davis looks back at me. "We will not give up until we have back what is rightfully ours. It matters not what you do, ape."

I don't know what to say to that, so I complete the knock sequence and the smooth metal surface of the spaceship irises open behind me. I don't turn around, but sit on the soft surface of the spaceship's interior and back myself in, brandishing the ultrasonic gizmo and squirt.

Bette Davis lowers her body, getting ready to pounce, but Charlie Chaplin is quicker. The little cat spins around, bounds two steps, and bowls the bigger Siamese down. He then runs two more quick steps and launches himself at me.

When the movement started, I dropped my squirt gun and started rapping the close sequence on the inside of the ship. The one Angelica Huston taught me. But my head does the math, projecting Charlie Chaplin's path and the speed with which the iris will close. There's a good chance the little guy will get chopped in half, so I hesitate.

And then Bette Davis is moving again and the little cat hits me in the chest and I go down. I tap once more on the hull and the ship closes up and I hear a soft bang on the other side as the Siamese bounces off.

"I did it, I did!" Charlie Chaplin says from my chest, a brief purr of happiness rumbling through his body. "I fooled 'em all. And here we are, governor. We got the ship. Now let's do this!"

What the hell is he talking about?

CHAPTER FORTY-SEVEN

SO, it turns out that cats aren't very sensitive to the human aging process. They can smell much better than we can, but their sight isn't as good.

But I don't think that's all of it. I don't think it's a distinction that matters to them. How old we are, that is. They just don't care. They want their sun patch and their food and their time stalking birds. Well... most cats. The ones I'm dealing with want me to take them back to Vega and back in time to restore their rightful place in the universe.

And, yes, I know it feels like I've wandered off into another long tangent, but this is actually important. I'm dealing with alien telepathic canines and felines, how they perceive us evolved apes is relevant.

So back to Charlie Chaplin crowing about how he "fooled 'em all."

"What's going on?" I ask, my time-travel beleaguered brain trying to catch up.

"Oh come on there, Ash," Charlie says, his chest still rumbling in a purr. I pet his slim body without even thinking about it and he settles down on my chest, the rumble gaining intensity. "I did as ya told me to. I got with this gang. I found ya like ya said I would. I told 'em all you was the Deliverer, I did. Charlie Chaplin did good, didn't he?"

"Yes," I say as I continue to pet him. The purr calming me down despite the fact there was a cat recently attached to my groin and I'm lying in the entryway of a time-traveling spaceship I just stole. "You did great, Charlie Chaplin. I am so proud of you."

I pause, petting him as my brain finally catches up as I figure out that a future version of me told Charlie Chaplin what to do and he's not getting that I am not that person yet.

It's stunning what a good job he did fooling me into thinking we had never met. Is this a quality of cats or just my general gullibility level when it comes to dealing with telepathic alien animals?

He nuzzles my hand with his head and I resume petting him. What do I do now? Pretend I'm the Ash that sent him on his mission, or tell him the truth and correct his misperception and see what he knows.

Maybe Charlie Chaplin is how I time bubble all of this in.

And then I remember the ruckus outside and the slamming door and the barking dogs.

"We need to get out of here," I say as I sit up and the cat gracefully jumps to the floor.

"It smells like dog in here, it does," he says in my head. "Not pleasant, not pleasant at all. Really not sure what ya see in that lot."

I don't answer but crawl to the bridge, once again appreciating the soft grey surfaces of the ship's interior. It's made for dogs, so there is no way I can stand up.

The little black cat pads along besides me but pauses at some small holes in the curved side of the passageway. "Humans are approachin', they are," he says. "Best we get outta here before they see the ship."

I crawl faster but make a mental note. Whatever smell language the dogs are using in their ships, the cats can understand. Both types of animals have very well-developed olfactory facilities.

But wait. Is "animals" the right word? Well, only if we evolved apes are also animals. And in the common vernacular where "animals" is a more generic term for biological beings that are driven more by instinct and reaction than intelligence, I guess we are. Just look around at this world.

I get to the bridge and make my way to the raised platform that has four holes that Angelica Huston puts her paws in. I've done this before. I practiced with the corgi. Inside are controllers suited to dog pads that can detect changes in pressure.

I use three fingers and a thumb in the front two holes and do as I practiced.

The grainy black-and-white display comes to life and I can see the yard and the white house. I do the sequence Angelica taught me and the ship lurches into the air, rather ungracefully, I might add.

Not that I can feel it. The inertial dampeners, or whatever tech they are employing, makes it feel like we aren't moving at all. It's the view screen, I can tell that the ship lurches into the air and then lists to the side before shooting up into the sky.

"Not so good at that, are ya?" Charlie Chaplin says in my head.

"No," I say. I'm sweating despite the perfect temperature inside the ship.

"I could take over, I could," Charlie Chaplin says.

"What?" I ask. The view screen shows Seattle dropping rapidly below us.

"Since we actually just met and all, I never had time to tell ya my full resumé," he begins, looking quite proud of himself. "I am a feline pilot, first class, I am. These canine ships ain't that different. I'm a bit small, so I'll need your help on the back controllers, but I can help."

I look back to the screen and focus until the curve of the Earth is visible, until we are high enough for a time jump. And then I carefully take my fingers off the controller and turn to Charlie Chaplin.

"I think we need to have a talk."

CHAPTER FORTY-EIGHT

THE CAT IS STARING at me, his adorable white mustache twitching as he sniffs me. The grainy black-and-white screen of the canine time-traveling spaceship shows the curve of the Earth and the North American continent below.

The ship is, once again, suffuse with complex smells that I can't make out and end up overwhelming my nose.

I just told Charlie Chaplin that on the street a day ago was the first time that I met him. His yellow eyes are fixed on me as his nose works. But he is not saying anything.

And then I have a thought that makes my stomach turn despite the perfectly inertial-dampered ride we just took into low orbit. What if it really was the first time we both met? What if Charlie Chaplin is a double agent and now trying to fool me? What if he is the backup plan, sent by Bette Davis in case I didn't do what they wanted?

But what can this adorable little cat do to me by itself?

His eyes aren't perfectly yellow, which I hadn't noticed

before. Around the vertical irises is a little bit of green, giving him a wilder look.

I'm sitting on the low pedestal and he is on the soft floor, the usually talkative cat silent.

"Are you okay?" I ask. I try not to be obvious, but look down to the pocket of my duster and realize that my ultrasonic gizmo isn't there. I left it right inside the ship's hatch.

Not that it seemed to bother him at all. Wait. Why didn't it bother him?

"Wait," he says, his voice slow, much slower than usual. "Are you sayin' that you just met me, but I met ya long ago when I was just a wee kitten? When ya rescued me from that horrible place?"

I rescued Charlie Chaplin? And what does "long ago" mean to a cat? "That is what I am saying."

"Huh!" he says, cocking his head to the side. "Well that's why ya was all crazy when you dropped me off back there. All, 'Listen to me, Charlie Chaplin, ya must not give any indication that ya know me. Ya must pretend I don't know ya are a fine pilot and we are best friends. Ya must pretend to hate dogs, knowin' that a few are quite fine. It'll be a fun game, it will.'"

First of all, that cat does a horrible impression of me. I don't sound like that. Secondly, either Charlie Chaplin is the real Deceiver or all of this just got a whole lot more complicated. Like me finding him and raising him and preparing him for what we are doing now. And him being my best friend.

But what are we doing now?

I groan and slide off the low platform and lie down on the soft surface of the bridge. "I hate time travel," I say.

"Oh, I can see that, Ash," he says. "It messes with your mind, it does. Everybody's what and when getting all mixed up like a pile o' newborn kits."

But if I can create the time bubble, the how of Charlie Chaplin doesn't really matter. Nothing really matters. That's why I am Evil Ash right now—the ends justify the means.

But what are the means?

That cat jumps on my chest, lies down, and starts purring. "I missed ya, I did," he says. "You are my ape."

I pet him and his purr deepens. This doesn't seem to be faked. Is the future me a dog person and a cat person?

"What did we do?" I ask as I pet him. "Before you started your mission back there?"

He sits up on my chest. "Oh, we had adventures, we did. Crazy adventures. But ya told me I was not to breathe a word of them. Not a word. That ya would have a heavy burden on your head when we met again and I was not to make it more complicated."

"Crazy adventures" sounds just like time travel.

"Damnit," I say.

"What's wrong?" he says in my head. "Charlie Chaplin can help, he can."

I have doubts. He seems to get more mixed up by time travel than I do. Or maybe he just lives firmly in the moment. In either case it doesn't seem like he can help, but maybe talking about it will.

So I spill it all. I sit up and hold him in my lap as I stare at the grainy view of the Earth below and I tell him about Mia and the whole adventure with Angelica Huston. About me wanting to right that wrong and the horrible mess it became in that time-bubbled incident. I tell him that I want to time bubble this all in so that I can go back to being a normal person.

I'm no longer wondering if the little cat is a double agent and I'm certainly treating him as a best friend. It feels good to let it all out.

I sigh and lie down and the little cat curls against my chest.

"But what about you and me?" he asks. "That's what I want to know. What happens to me after all this is sealed in a fancy timey bubble? I'll be stuck in the terrible place, won't I? You won't come rescue me, will ya?"

My heart is heavy, but I'm tired of lying so I tell him the truth. "No, Charlie Chaplin, I won't."

The cat doesn't say anything, just remains a warm comforting ball of fur next to me and I fall asleep.

CHAPTER FORTY-NINE

SO I CAN ONLY IMAGINE what you must think of me. Wanting to seal away all of this time travel and knowing intelligent alien life exists and knowing Angelica Huston and Charlie Chaplin.

Well... I know what I am thinking. Why the hell would a widowed sci-fi geek like me throw this away? Why would what happened in the time bubble with Mia be so bad that I would feel the need to seal it in again? I mean, it's already in a time bubble and it is not something that this version of me experienced directly. Why does it matter?

Angelica Huston trusts me. She showed me how to use her ship, preprogrammed those jumps in, not so I could time bubble myself in but so I could make a Möbius strip of causality of the stealing and giving back of her ship. And what about Charlie Chaplin? There is a bond I feel with the little guy that is undeniable.

But here's the thing. Mia was my life. My whole life.

Meeting her, being her partner, made my life worth living. And, yeah, I get that sounds super dramatic and all, but for an introverted geek like me, she was the reason behind everything.

And she died.

I know, I know, everyone dies. We all have to let go of what we care about the most... eventually. But it came so soon with her. It was hard, so hard, but I was adapting to it. Back in Phoenix looking after my parents, living a lonely life, but slowly healing. And then Angelica Huston came along and proved to me time travel is real as we traipsed through Mia's life and as I was her guardian angel.

This tore something open in me. A possibility. A hope. Of seeing Mia again. Of being there for her last rally. And "tore" is the right word here.

I tore my rotator cuff in my thirties—forgive the digression, it won't last long—playing disc golf. The nerdy version of golf, you will notice. It hurt like hell but wasn't bad enough for me to need surgery. The orthopedic surgeon I went to told me I'd be fine as long as I didn't reinjure it, so I should be careful with it.

I asked him what would happen if I did reinjure it. He said it would take surgery and a long and painful recovery requiring a lot of PT. That my arm would probably never be the same.

I can never recover from Mia's death. It's just not possible. She was my life. And what the time traveling with Angelica Huston did was reinjure the wound. Tore it right open. Made it so much worse than before. I need surgery and a time bubble is the only thing I can do to make this right.

And, I agree. It is selfish of me. It is not something Mia would have approved of, and it's not the kind of thing I would have ever considered if she was still with me, still alive.

But I am not whole and the only way I can think of to deal with this damage is a time bubble. Lock this version of me away and let Ashton Bach, the person I was before all of this, go on with his lonely life. Let him go on healing.

Not to mention what I experience during time jumps and whatever is going on in my limbic lobe. Time travel may be a deadly pursuit for me. My life may depend on me doing this.

When I wake up from my nap, my head full of self-recriminating thoughts, I find that Charlie Chaplin is staring at me. He's on the low control platform and for a moment I'm worried that he did something while I was asleep. That he is the world's most convincing double agent. That I was so stupid to trust him.

"I'll help ya," he says quietly in my head. "I'll help ya, Ash. I will. Ya saved me, and no matter what happens with this bubble thingy, nothing changes that. So, I'll help ya."

I sit up and try to put a smile on my face but the effort seems to loosen something in me and I cry. I'm a sci-fi geek in an alien bone-shape spaceship orbiting the Earth and I just cry. Like a baby.

I don't deserve Charlie Chaplin. I completely misjudged him. I never imagined that a feline would be my friend, much less give up his rescue, let it be time bubbled in, essentially give up his life for me.

And the cat doesn't do anything as the tears come and the sobs wrack my body. He sits there and stares. He is silent. He is witness.

He doesn't try to stop the tears. He doesn't try to make it better. He just sits there and lets me get it out. And then after it dies down, he crawls into my lap and starts purring and I feel so much calmer.

"You're a good cat, Charlie Chaplin," I say with a sniff as I rub my runny nose on the sleeve of my duster.

"That I am," he says in my head. "That I am."

CHAPTER FIFTY

THE SOLUTION IS SIMPLE. I can't time bubble myself in, but my friends can. Charlie Chaplin can. Angelica Huston can. And if Charlie is the one time bubbling me in, he goes on. He will be a time anomaly—not sure that is the right word for it—a product of a time that is locked away.

After I clean up, wipe the snot off my face, Charlie Chaplin and I get to work. He puts his paws in the front holes on the low platform on Angelica Huston's time-traveling spaceship. The stalk rises and stops in front of his nose, emitting data via smell that he can understand.

I tell him about the jumps that are preprogrammed in. I tell him how to trigger them.

And yes, there is a lingering sliver of a doubt, but it is so slim. I have to trust the cat so I might as well start trusting him now. And given my scratch-filled history with his species, this is something. The power of his affection and kindness has overcome my history with cats.

"First jump," I say. "We do a near pass on a past version of this ship, knocking it into a parallel world."

The cat looks at me and stares. I'm honestly not used to reading the expressions on cats faces. The one I'm used to seeing is "I'm going to scratch you now, you evil oaf." But I'd have to say it's the equivalent of a feline WTF expression. His eyes narrowed and his head slightly cocked.

"It already happened to me," I say with a shrug. "So it needs to happen again. Here's the sequence you need to do." And I tell him.

The cat is much smaller than the corgi. His paws seem to be swimming in those holes and his legs are awkwardly splayed to reach them both. But it's not a difficult maneuver since the sequence is preprogrammed. His paws only reach the front two holes, but the sequences only involve the front two controllers since Angelica set them up for an ape like me.

"Right, then. Here we go," he says, his paws moving and his nose twitching as he takes in the scents from the little stalk.

The grainy black-and-white display changes. We are diving down towards the Earth and then we are zooming up, the display dominated by the sun. And then the sun shudders, goes out of focus and my skin prickles, my stomach does somersaults, and I smell burning plastic.

An alarm goes off... well, I think it's an alarm. There is a smell, a musky smell, that is strong enough to break through my overpowered nose and I hear a high-pitched sound just at the edge of my hearing.

Charlie Chaplin is focused. His eyes on the screen and his nose twitching. The display wheels around and I see a flash, a brief image of a bone-shaped craft against the dark void of space and then I see the Earth again and then the whole Earth shudders and goes out of focus and I itch again, smelling burning plastic—it's even worse this time—and the Earth shudders again and comes back into focus and I am left sitting on the bridge and panting, sweat prickling on my neck.

"What the 'ell happened to you?" Charlie Chaplin asks.

I shrug. "Turns out time travel isn't really good for me."

He gives me another look. This one is similar, eyes narrowed and head cocked, but it's got more of a "I don't think I know you" vibe to it rather than WTF. It's a WTF variant, to be sure. I guess there is a lot I didn't tell the little guy when I rescued him.

Which I'm not planning to do anymore, so he is already a time anomaly. And if this developing plan succeeds, then Angelica Huston will never meet me and I am a time anomaly too.

And then I realize my colossal mistake. The twisting of time-travel logic is hard to follow, but I don't think I thought this time bubble thing through properly—and it's not like Angelica Huston sat me down and gave me a course in time-travel mechanics.

I thought my sci-fi geekery had supplied me with all I needed, but I was wrong.

Let me explain.

Let's go back to the first me, the one that got to see Mia during her rally, and it went horribly bad. Well, Angelica Huston did something to that me... returned me home, I would guess, and then time traveled back further and got to me before she had previously.

All the me's there are confusing. Let's try that a different way.

Let's call the first time-traveling me A1, and the me I am now is A2, and the me I am trying to go back to, the one that knows nothing of all this madness, A0.

So, Angelica Huston returned A1 home, time traveled back and created A2 when we hopped through Mia's young life and the wound of my grief was torn back open.

What happened to A1? Is he back in his apartment? Did it never burn down? Is he seeing a therapist to deal with the reinjured grief, with knowing he gave Mia a horrible experience right at the end of her life?

And by extension, when I have Charlie Chaplin and Angelica Huston time bubble me in, what happens to me, the A2 me? They drop me back in Phoenix, I go back to my parents' house pretending everything went fine in Seattle and try to get back to my life knowing everything I know.

If that is not a parallel world, then what is it? Do the A1 and the A2 versions of me just disappear? And the A1 version of Mia that had the horrible experience, did she disappear? Is the only record of that the video that Angelica Huston showed me of the A1 version of me freaking the hell out?

"Do you know about time bubbles?" I ask the cat, who is still staring at me with a gentler version of that WTF look.

"Oh, Charlie Chaplin is quite versed in time-travel mechanics," he says, puffing his chest out. "All felines are, ya know. Our feline minds are well suited to its twisting conundrums unlike ya apes."

"So you know what a time bubble is?" I ask.

"Oh sure. That's pretty simple stuff, as time travel goes."

"Can you tell me what it is?" I ask. "Exactly how it works."

He cocks his head the other way, like he is reevaluating me. "Sorry, Ash. Ya told me not to. But ya did tell me I could tell ya if you was on the right track."

I shake my head. Stupid time-travel rules. "Okay," I say with a sigh. "The only difference between a time bubble and a parallel universe is that a time bubble is transient. It's a minor change in the timeline, one that time can heal over. And when it is healed over, everyone and everything that is different about it is gone... forever."

I sit there blinking. The thought wasn't whole until I uttered it and it's a hell of a thought.

Now the cat looks shocked. I mean, his eyes wide "I can't believe you said that" shocked.

"That's right," he says. "I guess you are a pretty smart ape, after all."

This makes me feel so much better. The version of Mia that had the horrible experience of her rally is gone. Just an echo.

And then this totally freaks me out. I mean, hello, existential crisis time. By doing this, I will be erasing myself.

This version of myself, that is. A1 is gone forever, and if we do this, A2 will be gone forever.

Poof. Gone. Vamoose. Nothing here matters. Nothing A2 does matters. Nothing A2 experiences is really real.

And I'm A2, thus the existential crisis.

CHAPTER FIFTY-ONE

THAT ANY OF this is a surprise seems rather silly in retrospect. I blame it on our ape brain deficiency with time travel. As a species, we humans have a tough time with time. I mean, we have trouble being in the moment, being in the here and now, always thinking about the past or the future. How the hell are we to understand the intricacies of time travel?

And I think the term "time bubble" is a little misleading. It makes it seem like it is a snow-globe-like structure, that moment existing frozen, not healed over and gone forever.

I sit there chewing on my lip, wishing I could stand up and pace. I need to think and I need to move to think.

I don't know if you've ever had an existential crisis. It's that moment when you realize that you are just a blink in the cosmic tapestry of life and you wonder whether anything you do has any meaning.

Except if I succeed, this will be literally true. For the me that I am now.

And I get it, all my Evil Ash rambling, about the ends justifying the means and none of this matters because it's a time bubble was a clear sign that some part of me knew what a time bubble really was. And that I was embracing it.

Add to that my goal is to restore Ashton Bach, a version of me that was never touched by this, then a part of me definitely got it. A part of me knew. A part of me wanted it. But now this has—ummm—bubbled up to my conscious brain and this is starting to feel like a bizarre form of suicide.

I don't use that word lightly. And, yes, this is not the same thing as taking a fist full of pills and lights out forever. Ashton Bach, the A0 version of me, will go on. But me, A2, and all that is different between me and A0 will be gone. Forever. And none of this really matters.

The perfectly climate-controlled spaceship suddenly feels hot and the low roof feels like it's closing in on me. I am sweating, everywhere this time, and my heart is thumping like a jackhammer in my chest. The soft surface below me doesn't feel comforting anymore and my chest is tight, so tight.

"I need to get out of here," I gasp. "I need air... I need..."

I am suddenly a caged animal looking for escape.

I don't matter. Nothing matters. I will be gone soon.

I crawl around the low platform on the bridge of the spaceship towards the door and then I stop. We are in space. I can't get out.

I turn around and the tuxedo cat is there.

"Ya matter, Ash," he says in my head. He doesn't say it loud and it's a very short sentence for the loquacious cat. But it stops me.

I'm on all fours facing him. My head is down and his is held high so we are almost nose to nose.

"Ya matter to me, Ash," he says.

The cat somehow knows what I'm going through. Do all cats get the terrifying agony of a full-blown existential crisis? Is this something they've mastered, allowing them to happily sun most of the day and let humans serve them, pick up after them, pamper them?

"I do?" I ask. My voice is higher than usual and I sound like a child.

He steps forward and rubs his head against my chin, a gentle purr rumbling out of him.

"Ya do," he says. "Ya rescued me, ya did. Nothin' can ever change that. We both get time bubbled in, we both disappear in time, and ya still rescued me. Ya still saved me."

He told me this before, but it didn't quite sink in.

I nod as he continues to rub his face against my head. "I rescued you..." I mumble. Although this version of me hasn't... but it can.

I sit down and scoop the little cat up. "Tell me where and when I rescued you. And that's what I'll be doing when the time bubble reabsorbs me. I'll be rescuing you, Charlie Chaplin. I'll be taking care of you."

The cat doesn't speak, but the rumble of his purr speaks volumes.

CHAPTER FIFTY-TWO

TIME REABSORBS US ALL. Whether we are locked in a time bubble or not. Our end comes. We are forgotten. What is left of us is the love and the kindness we do.

I know. Sappy, right? Right out of a Hallmark card or something. I don't know if that's useful or not, but it's what is always on the other end of an existential crisis. For me, at least. Just because there is an end doesn't mean that what we do doesn't matter.

It does. It has to.

As I hold the purring cat, as the existential crisis fades, I come to accept my inevitable end. Imperfectly, I might add. We apes aren't really wired to imagine a world without us—thus the whole existential crisis in the first place.

And as I accept my end and as I accept that the small things matter, I realize that Evil Ash is gone.

What I do matters. Even in a time bubble. The ends never justify the means.

Right. So more sappy stuff from Ashton Bach. I am what I am, and if all this madness has proved anything to me, it's that I'm okay with who I am. All my lanky, middle-aged, big-nosed geekiness.

Maybe it's the cat trusting me, purring in my lap. Maybe it's the corgi trusting me and waiting for me to return her ship. Maybe it's having the adventure of a lifetime when I thought that without Mia my life was essentially over.

I don't know. I'm not one to look a gift cat, or a gift dog, in the mouth.

I'm not sure how long we are like that. For once I am fully in the moment and time slips past without me really noticing much. I think this is the power of the cat. They seem to have a completely different relationship with time than we apes.

At some point, the cat crawls off my lap, stretches, and asks, "What's next there, Ash?"

"It's time to return the ship," I say. "It's time to do this."

The black cat sits and licks his white paw and starts washing his face. "I've been thinkin', I have," he says. "And I want to stay with ya, Ash. You goin' in a time bubble, then Charlie Chaplin is goin' in a time bubble. Let's get that dog to do the time bubbly thing."

My mouth opens, a thousand thoughts trying to rush out, but no words make it. Charlie is an intelligent, sentient being, and he can make his own choices.

I nod. "So we'll go rescue the younger you," I say.

"And every other cat we can until time heals over and reabsorbs us," he says, a fierce look in his yellow eyes. "And dogs too... if we must. I know ya like the dogs."

I smile and I realize that I am actually happy. Truly

happy. It's not saving the world and it's just a blip in a time bubble that will soon disappear. But it's something worth doing. It's something I want to do.

"Okay, then," I say. "Please man your post, pilot first-class Charlie Chaplin. We've got a mission and we best get to it."

CHAPTER FIFTY-THREE

CHARLIE CHAPLIN BRINGS the silver bone-shaped time-traveling spaceship to a gentle landing in Jessica Cole's backyard. He really is a good pilot, not just bravado from the little guy there.

I walk out onto the bouncy green grass and Angelica Huston is at the edge of the patio, her tail wagging shyly, her nose twitching as she smells me.

It's an odd moment, and it's not the kind of greeting I'm used to with a dog. Maybe she smells that cat. Maybe she wasn't sure of me and my intentions.

But it's only a moment and then she is barking happily and bounding towards me. I squat down and soon have a bundle of corgi in my lap as she enthusiastically licks my face.

"I missed you, Ash," she says in my head, and I am so glad to hear her voice, with her finely cultured British accent. "You don't seem damaged, my ape friend. How did you get away from that clowder of cats?"

Ahh... there it is. "Clowder" is the right term for a group of cats, although "murder" certainly fits that group a lot better.

"I'm sorry, Angelica Huston," I say. "That I was like that. I'm sorry they scared you. I... I was going through something."

"Oh, say nothing of it, Ash," she says in my head. "You brought my ship and all is right with the world now."

I hear the sound of someone clearing their throat, but it's in my head and it sounds like it's coming from behind me. Which is weird, because it's the telepathic tuxedo cat making himself known.

The corgi stiffens in my lap, a low growl emanating from deep in her chest.

"Angelica Huston," I begin. "I'd like you to meet Charlie Chaplin."

The corgi's growl deepens and she tries to leap out of my lap up into the ship where the cat is, but I hold her tight. Barely. The dog is quite strong.

Behind me Charlie hisses and I get the impression that they are talking to each other. Probably throwing insults and cursing.

"Don't be rude, you two," I say. "Let me hear what you are saying. And be nice. You are both my friends."

"...and he rescued me, he did," Charlie Chaplin is saying. "When I was but a wee kit. He rescued me from a terrible place and he saved me and that makes him my ape, it does."

"Is this true, Ash?" she asks. The dog has relaxed so I let her go and she walks back several steps and stares at me and the cat behind me.

I nod. "I believe it is. A future version of me will do it." The little cat jumps on my shoulder.

"And you are his ape?" she asks. Her tone is steady but I can hear the disappointment.

"I am my own ape, thank you very much," I say. "But you are both my friends. You are both my best friends."

"You watch her there, Ash," Charlie says in my head, and I get the impression he is just talking to me. "Her kind is devious and vicious. They'll turn on ya, they will. They'll bite the hand that feeds them, for sure."

"Ashton Bach," Angelica says in my head, and again I get the impression that her words are just for me. "Do not trust this feline. They are a devious race, always scheming. Always up to no good."

"Both of you, listen to me," I say, pulling Charlie Chaplin from my shoulder and setting him on the grass next to me. "I need you to—"

Angelica leaps at Charlie, barking and growling. Charlie runs and is up a tree before the dog can get close. Angelica barks her head off and the cat hisses from above.

I laugh. I have to. No matter how evolved a species gets, some things remain the same.

I TAKE a step to go do something about the animals, but Jessica Cole is there. She's dressed in the same black jeans and black sweater, her short, bleach-blond hair spiked up, her smile big enough to emphasize her wrinkles and her sixty-plus years.

She was twenty-three years younger the last time I saw her, when I attempted to create a Möbius strip of causality of her greeting of me a day ago. (In local time, not subjective time. Subjectively it feels like years although it's been only a few days.)

A smile is playing on her full lips as she looks me up and down.

I turn towards the cat and the dog. "Just let them be," she says. "They have to work it out."

I nod and look at her, she still looks to be six feet of sensuous badass. But it's a little different this time. I don't feel so intimidated. Maybe it's my brief stint as Evil Ash. Maybe it's the recent existential crisis.

"You could have told me," I say, referring to that Möbius strip of causality.

"And spoil the fun?" she asks.

I stare at her hoping for something more. Some assurances that her kiss on seeing me was just her doing what I told her to do. But I let that go. It doesn't really matter if we had/will have a relationship.

"I see your point," I say with a grin.

She looks me over again. "I suspect if I kissed you again it wouldn't be such a big deal."

I feel my cheeks flush, but only a bit. "The right kind of kisses are always a big deal," I say with a grin.

She laughs, it's brief and loud and it makes me want to hear her laugh some more. "Well... you have changed," she says. "Good. That will help with this next part."

"Next part?" I ask.

"Yeah," she says with a smile as she turns toward the house. "He wants to talk to you again."

CHAPTER FIFTY-FOUR

IN JESSICA'S KITCHEN, I notice a dog bowl. It's ceramic and a pale blue, filled to the rim with water, sitting on the tile floor. The kitchen is still spotless, all granite and stainless steel and red accents.

Jessica is back in the yard having told me that he is waiting in the living room. And by the time I walk into the kitchen, I know who "he" is.

"There's some fresh clothes in the bathroom," he says.

It's him. It's me. The seventy-something version of me with short-cropped steel-grey hair and a tanned and deeply wrinkled face with that diagonal scar that runs from the right side of his nose about an inch. He's older. Stronger. A lot more confident.

He's sitting on a simple black couch in Jessica's Zen living room. It's bright and sunny with a few plants, lots of wood, and lots of space.

I'm not really the same person I was when we met in Seattle, before I stole the ship, just a few hours ago, subjectively. But he's... he's very different from me and not just in years. I can see it clearly now. He's got the kind of easy confidence I've always longed for.

"Freshen up," he says, nodding towards the bathroom. "Always a good idea after a mission."

He, of course, knows that I need to freshen up. He knows that I pissed myself, just a little, when that cat was attached to my groin. I wonder if older, cooler Ash ever pisses himself.

"Thanks," I say.

"Sure," he says with a smile. "I'll pour us some drinks."

The bathroom is small with a white pedestal sink and a shower stall. On the sink is a set of clothes, the whole black jeans and sweater both Jessica and the older me seem to always be wearing.

I look in the mirror. My brown eyes look tired and I've got several days' growth of beard. But there's something else. Since Mia died what I always seemed to see was this scared, lonely man entering the last act of his life alone. I had taken to looking in the mirror as little as possible.

Now?

I'm not sure, but the face I'm looking at looks a little older, but less scared and less lonely.

There's a disposable razor and a new toothbrush on the sink and I take the hint. It's myself that's waiting on me, so I don't feel bad about taking some time. I take a shower. Shave. Brush my teeth. Just normal human stuff.

The clothes fit, of course, and when I come out into the

living room, older me is still there. He's gazing out the large picture windows and I follow his gaze and I see Charlie Chaplin chasing Angelica Huston, but it seems more playful than serious.

Jessica is out in the yard with them and watching and laughing. Then the dog turns and the cat runs away.

"They're good together," future-me says.

"Who?" I ask.

He looks at me, and I see something different in his brown eyes this time. Fatigue. Deep fatigue. Like he's seen a lot.

"Angelica Huston and Charlie Chaplin," he says with a mischievous grin.

He nods at an armless black chair that has a good view of the backyard and hands me a glass with two fingers of whiskey. I notice that his glass has about twice that.

We clink glasses and he takes a real sip while I take the smallest sip possible. The alcoholic tang is a shock at first but then the flavor and warmth comes through and I sigh and relax back into the chair.

"So...," he begins, "to time bubble or not to time bubble, that is the question."

"Is it?" I ask, his Shakespearean reference not lost on me. I wonder if it is intentional or just the reuse of a phrase that is part of our culture.

He smiles, it's full and free of irony. One bushy eyebrow shoots up. "It is. The choice is yours. I am content with my journey. Time bubble or no, it's been a hell of a ride."

He raises his glass and takes another sip.

"Of which you will tell me not one thing," I say.

He shakes his head. "Not one. Best you experience it for yourself."

"But not if there is a time bubble," I say. "I assume Angelica Huston will do it."

He nods. "If you make a convincing enough argument."

"In that case this is our time bubble and we'll fade away," I say.

He nods, looking back out at the yard. The dog and the cat are sitting close looking at each other. I have to imagine they are having a hell of a conversation.

"And if I don't," I say, "then we are full citizens of this timeline and there is no more Ashton Bach."

"No," he says. "Not after the telepathic corgi started talking to him. That was the beginning of the end of Ashton Bach."

He referred to the older version of us as "him." And I get that. It was only days ago that I was Ashton Bach, but I don't feel like him anymore.

I take another sip and just sit there. For once I don't feel like I'm in a hurry. Like there is work to be done or a timeline to be saved or something urgent that needs scurrying after.

"What about our parents?" I ask. "Someone needs to take care of them."

He just grins at me, and in that moment I really recognize myself. The grin is part excitement, part goofy, and all me. He doesn't need to say anything else.

"Time travel," I say for him.

He nods. "You can still be there for them." The grin melts away and he looks old again, and it's clear there was some trauma there. He has lost his parents. I haven't. It can't be easy.

"And you aren't going to tell me what you did," I say. It's not a question and my older self doesn't answer. "But aren't I going to do the exact same thing that you did?" I ask.

He shrugs. Casually. Like it doesn't matter at all one way or the other. "Fate and free will exist together just fine," he says, still looking out at the yard. "You will do what you are fated to do and the choice will be yours."

"So it will be what you did," I say.

He shrugs again.

"You don't know or you don't care?" I ask, my tone rising.

He swivels towards me and leans forward. "Both. In regards to time travel there are a lot of things to understand. A lot of things that matter. Your whole obsession with Möbius strips of causality is not one of them. Whether you will do what I did, whether it's fate or free will... it just doesn't matter."

My jaw drops open and I chew on air for a few breaths trying to come up with the right words. "Then what the hell does matter?" I ask.

He turns back to the window and nods. Jessica is sitting on the grass with Angelica Huston and Charlie Chaplin. They appear to be having a conversation.

Does he mean that telepathic aliens matter? That friendships matter? That conversations matter?

I open my mouth to speak but he's getting up, his brown eyes intense. "Good luck, kid. And don't stress too much. All's well that ends well."

He walks out of the living room and down a hallway and I hear a door open and close and I swear I hear the low woof of a dog.

All's well that ends well.

He drops a direct Shakespearean reference this time and just left the room. What the hell?

I get up and march after him. The hallway is short, going just past the bathroom with a door on either side. I take the left one, which I figure is the master bedroom.

I open the door and move to step in but stop short.

The older me is on the floor with an older dog. A corgi. She has the same radar ears and tan-and-white coat as the dog I was just looking at in the backyard, but her eyes are dull and her coat is thin and she is quite a bit heavier.

She thumps her tail and looks at me with those deep soul-searching brown eyes of hers. But there is something different there.

She waddles over and I get down and pet her. She gets in my lap and licks my face. She knows me and I know her, I am clear about that, but something is different.

"Angelica Huston," I say. "Look at you, such a pretty girl, even at your age."

She doesn't reply and it hits me what is different about her.

I look up at my future-self and I think I understand what I saw in his eyes. Not sadness. At least, not just sadness. Something a lot more complicated than that.

"She..." I begin, swallowing hard. "She's just a dog now."

He nods. "But 'just' is the wrong word. She's fully in service now, which she wanted more than anything."

I can't see the future, but there is enough of me in my future-self for me to understand. This version of me helped Angelica Huston become a "normal" dog, accepting a limit to her intelligence and a shortened lifespan. Angelica Huston told me this was the highest level of achievement for one of her kind.

"Don't be sad, kid. She got her wings," he says.

And now a reference to *It's a Wonderful Life*. It seems the older me pulls out a wider range of pop culture references, not just sci-fi and fantasy.

And I realize a few other things. This version of me is with Jessica Cole. They are all here retired caring for Angelica Huston. All their time-traveling adventures are over.

"Do you miss it?" I ask.

He shrugs again. Something of a habit for him. "Of course. But I am grateful for a simple life too." He nods at the corgi in my lap. "I'd do anything for her."

"And Charlie Chaplin?" I ask, nodding towards the back of the house. "All's well that ends well there?"

My older self nods. "Just like the play, things get pretty complicated, but he lands on his feet just fine."

I sit there petting the old corgi who is soon snoring softly in my lap. This older me is clearly not in a rush and it seems to be rubbing off.

Even though I know Angelica Huston's dream was to be like this, to be a normal dog and to be fully in service, it's hard for me to come to terms with. She went from being a time-traveling telepathic canine to being a bit of an oversized lap dog.

And as I think about it, that sounds stupid. The dogs in

my life had improved it on so many levels. At times they were really the only thing that made my life worth living, that got me up in the morning.

So there is a race of telepathic aliens that consider service more valuable than intelligence or longevity.

Well... that doesn't sound quite right, either. Most dogs I know have a higher emotional intelligence than most people I know. Intelligence isn't just one thing.

I look up at my older self and he has a small compassionate smile on his face. He must remember what this moment was like.

"I'm happy for her, but... I'm sad too," I say.

He nods. "That's kinda life, kid." He sighs and gets up with a groan. "Take your time. Make your decision. No pressure."

He walks out of the room and closes the door.

The bedroom has a queen bed, an oak dresser, and a few pictures on the wall. But I don't remember much about it. It is the corgi that holds my attention as she breathes deeply, her paws twitching as she runs in her dream.

I have to wonder if the dream is one of her time-traveling adventures or just something more mundane like chasing a squirrel.

All the craziness since I met the younger, more alien version of this corgi seems to fade in that moment. All those breathless moments and twisting logic and hard decisions just pale in comparison to this quiet moment with this old dog.

My existential crisis that was ruling my mind just an hour or two ago seems silly. Of course it all ends. Of course time takes so much away from us. But if we can have moments like this, then it all makes sense.

Without thinking, without worrying, as I pet the sleeping corgi, I know what I want.

I hear a bark from outside and the muffled sound of Jessica's laughter and I just smile.

EPILOGUE

HERE'S the thing about the time bubble that I was so desperate for. It was all about me. My freak out about what Mia experienced when I tried to right the wrong of missing her rally. The wound that was Mia's death getting ripped back open. My being overwhelmed by this whole time travel thing, which can get, admittedly, rather crazy.

Me. Me. Me.

Having a sleeping corgi in my lap that had given up so much just to be in service in the most pure way possible wakes me up to that.

It is the power of the dog. At least for me. They love so purely, they live in the moment, they forgive in an instant.

Cats... well, they are a little more complicated, but I am coming to learn that the love and trust of a cat is a hell of a thing too.

My epiphany isn't earth shattering or anything. It is simply this. I want to be more like a dog. I want to be in the moment. I want to be of service to others. I want to be playful and happy and content with what I have.

I know. It is a lot for us evolved apes to shoot for. Dogs seem to be wired for it and we are not. But I can learn.

The older Angelica Huston's nap is not that long. Maybe twenty minutes. And then she gets up, shakes, and stands at the door looking at it.

"Okay, girl," I say.

I let her out and she pads into the kitchen, gets a big drink, and with some effort hops on the couch and goes back to sleep.

I smile. The old corgi has given me my treatment, and with my epiphany in hand I have been dismissed. It's time for her to have a real nap.

I go to the sliding glass door and look out into the yard. The younger Angelica Huston is curled up next to Jessica who is sitting on the grass, her face pointed up to the sun which has broken through the clouds.

My older self is sitting at the wrought-iron table on the patio with a drink in front of him quietly watching the scene.

And Charlie Chaplin is sniffing around the silver bone-shaped spaceship, but lazily as if he expects nothing to come of it. Seeing him makes me wonder about Bette Davis and how much those cats long to go back to Vega, go back to the past and right a wrong.

What they *perceive* as a wrong. Boy did I learn that with the whole Mia rally thing.

I look back at the old Angelica and then the young Angelica. They look almost the same as they sleep, their radar ears still up, listening, ready to leap into action.

I miss Mia. It's an ache that I don't expect will ever go away. My grieving for her has been ripped wide open. But maybe that's for the best. Maybe it will heal a little bit better this time, but I expect it will always be a problem.

From this vantage, I can see a bit of the scar on the older me's head. It's straight and I have to wonder if he had surgery to deal with whatever is going on with my (and his) temporal lobe and time travel.

Maybe it's not just age and a desire to be with Angelica Huston in her old age that grounded him.

And Jessica Cole. Beautiful and intriguing at any age. But so not my type. So not Mia. But I really think there is something there between her and my older self. It's hard to imagine being with anyone but Mia, but after all of this it seems like something worth imagining.

I smile, take one last look at the older Angelica Huston, and open the sliding glass door and step outside into my future.

WANT MORE ANGELICA AND ASH?

MY WRITING PROCESS is an odd one. I follow my gut and my heart. I write across many genres and series. Writing is my "me time," so I go with the flow as much as possible.

It's clear there's a ton more story that could be written here and if you want to read it, you can influence my process. Make your voice heard. Leave a review wherever you buy books. Tell a friend (or twenty). Talk about it on social media. Or reach out to me directly, which you can do over on my website at: RobertJMcCarter/contact.

And sign up for my newsletter at RobertJMcCarter/newsletter, that way you'll know the moment there is another Angelica and Ash story to read.

If you're not familiar with my work and are looking for something similar, I don't have anything else quite like this right now. I do have a couple other series that are a bit quirky and rather playful with their genres and ideas. Here's just a little bit about them:

WOODY AND JUNE VERSUS THE APOCALYPSE

A story of adventure and love and taking things (even the apocalypse) in stride.

A little bit "The Walking Dead" mixed with the adventurous spirit of "Romancing the Stone" set in the rugged landscape of the Arizona desert. It's romance, action, adventure, and humor... and more fun than an apocalypse has a right being.

You can grab ebooks for the first two episodes for free by signing up for the Woody and June fan club at WoodyAndJune.com

NEUTRINOMAN & LIGHTNINGIRL: A LOVE STORY

Superheroes... falling in love... saving the world

Follow Nik Nichols (aka Neutrinoman) and Licia Lopez (aka Lightningirl) on this wild adventure past "happily ever after" into the heart of love while they try to protect the Earth from aliens bent on our destruction.

The ebook for the first episode, *Meteor Attack!* is free when you sign up for my newsletter at RobertJMcCarter/newsletter

I have several other series and lots of other books. Find out more at RobertJMcCarter.com

ACKNOWLEDGMENTS

The origin of this story is pretty interesting (as I bet you can imagine), but I don't have room to write about that here. I will give you the very short version: It was on the rim of the Grand Canyon in January of 2019. It had snowed eight inches the night before and the canyon was at its most spectacular. My wife and I, grieving the loss of our spaniel Madison, met an older corgi named Aspen trying valiantly to keep up with her person on her short little legs on the hard-packed snow. That environment and that dog led directly to the creation of Angelica Huston. Intrigued? There's more on my website at RobertJMcCarter.com/AngelicaOrigin

All of that background is to start this acknowledgement with thanks to Aspen for soothing our battered hearts and to the Grand Canyon for enveloping us in such beauty.

Angelica Huston made her first appearance in a short story called "Dog People" written for Snot-Nosed Aliens: Stories from Pulphouse Fiction Magazine. This is a story featuring Angelica Huston before she was a time traveler. The anthology has a lot of other fun stories and "Dog People" features the Grand Canyon as my wife and I saw it that January.

Big thanks to my first listener, cheerleader, partner, and true dog person, Aleia O'Reilly. None of these books happen without her. Thank you, my love.

Also big thanks to my indispensable pack of beta readers, Roni Hornstein, Peter Klein, and Eliot Schipper, and to my proofreader, Diana Cox. Thanks for making this book better.

And a thank you beyond words to all the four-legged companions that have graced my life and made it so very, very much better and made me a much better person. We have decided to donate at least 10% of the proceeds from this book to no-kill animal sanctuaries and organizations that help animals in need find a good home.

ABOUT THE AUTHOR

Robert J. McCarter is the author of over a dozen novels, nine novellas, and dozens of short stories. He is a finalist for the *Writers of the Future* contest and his stories have appeared or are forthcoming in *The Saturday Evening Post, Pulphouse Fiction Magazine, Fiction River, Andromeda Spaceways Inflight Magazine*, and numerous anthologies.

A recent effort is a serialized novel called *Woody and June Versus the Apocalypse*, a story of adventure and love and taking things (even the apocalypse) in stride. Of his novel, *Seeing Forever*, Kirkus Reviews says, "Sci-fi as it should be: engaging, moving, and grand in scope."

He lives in the mountains of Arizona with his amazing wife and his ridiculously adorable dogs.

Find out more at:
RobertJMcCarter.com

BOOKS BY ROBERT J. MCCARTER

ANGELICA AND ASH TIME TRAVEL ADVENTURES

- Where the Past Belongs

CARTERVILLE MYSTERIES

- **Out of a Christmas Sky**
- **Unnamed 2021 Novel**
- **The Blood of Carterville**

WALTER ANCHOR, GHOST DETECTIVE STORIES

- **Case 1: Detecting Haley** (also part of *Life After: Stories of Life, Death, and the Places in Between*)
- **Case 2: The Ghost Bride's Gift**
- **Case 3: A Long Hard Fall**
- **Case 4: Death of a Dentist**
- **Case 5: A Hollywood Kind of a Murder**
- **Case 6: The Red Arrow Murders**
- **Unfinished Business: The Cases of Walter Anchor Ghost Detective**

For a complete list of Walter Anchor stories, go to RobertJMcCarter.com/WalterAnchor

NOVELS IN THE "GHOST'S MEMOIR" WORLD:

- Shuffled Off: A Ghost's Memoir, Book 1
- Drawing the Dead
- To Be a Fool: A Ghost's Memoir, Book 2
- Of Things Not Seen: A Ghost's Memoir, Book 3
- A Boy, a Girl, and a Ghost

For a complete list the "Ghost's Memoir" novels, go to ShuffledOff.com

THE WOODY AND JUNE VERSUS THE APOCALYPSE SERIES

Find out more at WoodyAndJune.com

THE NEUTRINOMAN AND LIGHTNINGIRL SERIES

Find out more at Neutrinoman.com

OTHER NOVELS:

- Seeing Forever

For a more information, go to RobertJMcCarter.com